Harold Pinter and the Self
Modern Double Awareness and Disguise
in the Shadow of Shakespeare

Harold Pinter and the Self
Modern Double Awareness and Disguise
in the Shadow of Shakespeare

Makoto Hosokawa

KEISUISHA
2016

About the author

MAKOTO HOSOKAWA is Professor of English at Chukyo University in Nagoya, Japan. He received his M.A. (1974) and Ph.D. (2004) from Hiroshima University. He studied Shakespeare at the Shakespeare Institute, University of Birmingham, 1985-86, and was a Visiting Professor in the School of English, Drama & American and Canadian Studies at the University of Birmingham, September 2009-January 2010. He is the author of *Kyo to Jitu no Hazama de: Shakespeare no Disguise no Keifu [Between Essence and Construct: The Genealogy of Disguise in Shakespeare]* (Tokyo: Eihosha, 2003).

Copyright © 2016 Makoto Hosokawa
Printed in Japan

ALL RIGHT REAERVED. No part of this work may be reproduced, redistributed, or used in any form or by any means without prior written permission of the publisher and copy-right owner.

Published by KEISUISHA co., ltd.
1-4 Komachi Naka-ku Hiroshima 730-0041 Japan

ISBN978-4-86327-336-8 C3098

Acknowledgments

I owe profound thanks to Christopher J. Armstrong for his reading of the manuscript and giving me invaluable comments and suggestions. I am also grateful to Susan Brock and Brian Crow for reading the original essay of the fourth chapter and giving me useful comments. I would also like to acknowledge the help of Mark Taylor-Batty, who referred me to Pinter's appearance in *The Taming of the Shrew* in his youth at the conference *Fractured Narratives: Pinter, Postmodernism and the Postcolonial World 5th-7th November 2009*, held at Goldsmiths, University of London.

I am thankful to the staff of the British Library where I consulted Harold Pinter Archive at various stages of my research. Thanks are also due to the Chukyo University Library and the University of Birmingham Library where I used their resources in the earlier stages of my work.

Last but not least my thanks should go to Chukyo University for providing me with a U.G.C. grant for the publication of this book.

The chapters of this book are revised versions of essays that appeared previously in the *Journal of the College of World Englishes* (Chukyo University):

"Double Awareness and the Self in Pinter's *The Collection* and *The Lover*" in vol. 11 (March, 2009).

"Unity and Division of the Self in *The Homecoming*: Against Two Kinds of Realism" in vol. 12 (March, 2010).

"The 'New' Modernity and Doubles in Harold Pinter's *No Man's Land*" in vol.13 (March, 2011).

"The Meaning of Rebecca's Disguise as a Dispossessed Mother in

Pinter's *Ashes to Ashes*" in vol.14 (March, 2012). An earlier version of this essay was presented at the 2011 M/MLA Convention, St. Louis Union Station Marriott, St. Louis Missouri on November 5, 2011. I would like to thank Lance Norman for valuable comments.

"Davies's Disguise in *The Caretaker*: From the Views of Modernist Negation and the Tradition of Disguise" in vol.15 (March, 2013).

"Pinter's *One for the Road, Party Time, Celebration* and Power's Invisibility: From Shakespearian Disguise to Postmodern Subject" in vol. 16 (March, 2014).

"Stanley's Ambiguous Self and Destiny: From the Modes of Representation and the Disguise Motif in *The Birthday Party*" in vol.17 (March, 2015).

I thank the editors of the journal for permission to reprint these articles.

Table of Contents

Acknowledgements i

Introduction 1

1. Stanley's Ambiguous Self and Destiny: From the Modes of
   Representation and the Disguise Motif in *The Birthday Party* 9

2. Davies's Disguise in *The Caretaker*: From the Views of Modernist
   Negation and the Tradition of Disguise 33

3. Double Awareness and the Self in *The Collection* and *The Lover* ... 51

4. Unity and Division of the Self in *The Homecoming*:
   Against Two Kinds of Realism 67

5. The "New" Modernity and Doubles in *No Man's Land* 87

6. The Meaning of Rebecca's Disguise as a Dispossessed Mother
   in *Ashes to Ashes* 103

7. *One for the Road, Party Time, Celebration* and Power's Invisibility:
   From Shakespearian Disguise to Postmodern Subject 121

Works Cited 143

Index 151

Introduction

The Nature of Pinter's Plays

About the same time as Harold Pinter wrote *The Collection* (1961) and *The Lover* (1962), he wrote, "I'd say that what goes on in my plays is realistic, but what I'm doing is not realism" ("Writing for Myself" 11), after insisting, "I'm convinced that what happens in my plays could happen anywhere, at any time, in any place, although the events may seem unfamiliar at first glance" ("Writing for Myself" 11). This comment is very convincing and fits our often perplexed first impressions of his plays, intimating how they really are, paradoxically realistic and anti-realistic or illusory. As John Russell Taylor puts it, "the language which the characters use is an almost uncannily accurate reproduction of every day speech. . . . and yet . . . the whole external world of everyday realities is thrown into question" (325-26). Is this characteristic of his plays to be attributed to Pinter's own artistic idiosyncrasy or to something else? This problem seems to be connected with Pinter's own position within trends in thought and literature since the nineteenth century.

As for Pinter's enigmatic or paradoxical language regarding his plays ("realistic," "not realism," "unfamiliar"), modern double awareness seems to explain the ambiguity explicitly, and illuminate what Pinter's plays are like. There is, in fact, no doubt that he himself shares the double awareness, for, he says, "We will all interpret a common experience quite differently, though we prefer to subscribe to the view that there's a shared common ground, a known ground. I think there's a shared common ground all right, but that it's more like a quicksand" ("Writing for the Theatre" 12).

Double Awareness and the 20th century Scientific World View

Many critics have noticed that there are both objectivism and subjectivism in Pinter's representation in general. The former comes from the realism of the nineteenth century, and the latter originates in modernism. Michael Bell calls such coincidence of the opposites "double awareness," which results from such modern scientific revolutions as the invention of the X ray or Heisenberg's 'Uncertainty principle.' He argues that such an awareness influences modern writers such as James Joyce and Thomas Man, who "use realist representation . . . yet with an X ray awareness of its constructed, or purely human, character" (12). This double awareness would explain Pinter's enigmatic definition of representation cited above. About the double awareness in Pinter's plays and *The Birthday Party* (1957), Varun Begley says that "early plays and late plays alike traverse a spectrum of realism and modernism" (38), "*The Birthday Party* . . . with one foot in the mundane and one in a cultural phantasmagoria" (45).

"The modern physicist," Michael Bell says, "continues to live in the Newtonian world of the layman while knowing its limited, almost illusory, character" (12) from the more scientific knowledge such as the X ray invented in 1895, and he points out the same double awareness of modern writers influenced by this. This awareness is implied in Harold Pinter's enigma about his plays of "the weasel under the cocktail cabinet" (qtd. in John Russell Taylor 323).

Franklin L. Baumer calls this revolution the "new" modernity, and says "The 'new' modernity . . . dispensed with being, leaving men without landmarks, casting them adrift on an endless sea of becoming" (402). According to Baumer, the "old" modernity from the seventeenth century "left important bastions of being virtually intact" (402), and though it bore another feature of the "Space-mind" which "produces a world of solid objects and absolutes that exist eternally" (403), the mind was replaced in the "new" modernity by the "Time-mind," which "sees everything *sub specie temporis*, as perpetually restless, moving, and changing" (402-03). Becoming and Time-mind are the key features of the "new" modernity and of modernism.

The "new" modernity started from a revolution in European thinking in the twentieth century, of which Heisenberg's 'Uncertainty principle' is representative. The new modernity produced "the new mentality" of "the famous three a's . . . the Absurd, anxiety, and alienation" (Baumer 414). In the world of the "new" modernity, the ideas of the objective and the absolute disappeared, "all realities have become subjective fictions" (Bradbury and McFarlane 27). The roaming and downtrodden Jenkins in *The Caretaker* (1959) is surrounded by this kind of absurd, existential and phenomenological atmosphere in which we find his identity also fittingly fictitious, due to disguise.

According to Bell, "The modernist decades were a time of epochal shift, like that of Shakespeare. . ." (12). It is true that Shakespeare lived in the days when a view of the world was shifting from the teleological idea of the chain of being to the mechanistic Newtonian view. Shakespeare also had a view of double awareness, which we call the 'Ancient' double awareness. This parallelism of double awareness is true of the view of man, too. In the era of Shakespeare, man is considered to be a microcosm which reflects the macrocosm, at the same time as man is being separated from the universe, and becomes an "independent being, in the sense that his or her paradigm purposes are to be found within, and not dictated by the larger order of which he or she is a part" (Charles Taylor 192-93).

Bell argues further that "Throughout much of the nineteenth century, natural science had been the paradigmatic form of truth statement" (11), having a great influence on naturalism and realism in literature. "Zola's naturalism . . . was the culminating example" (11). But around the turn of the century "science itself was losing some of its epistemological self-evidence" (11) due to "the recognition that science is a construction of the human mind before it is a reflection of the world" (11). Evidence presented by the newly invented X ray revealed the solid desk defined by natural science since Newton was not solid, but penetrable. Naturally, this shift in scientific thinking caused a departure from realism and representational verisimilitude in literature. But in spite of such a scientific shift, physicist Arthur Eddington, according to Bell, maintains that the "modern physicist . . . lives in two worlds at once" (Bell 12):

> He uses the same solid plane surface of the writing table as anyone else, but he also knows that the table is "really" a mass of moving particles through which, given the appropriate technique, it would be possible to penetrate without disturbance. (Bell 12)

The Self and Disguise in Pinter's Plays

As for the self, in the age of 'Ancient' double awareness, it has a multiplicity which reflects the ultimate One, like the Protean man in Pico della Mirandola's *Oration on the Dignity of Man* while it becomes the disengaged unitary self in Descartes's view. In view of literary theory of that period, the former reflects the idealism of neo-platonism, "idealist mimesis," while the latter reflects realism, "realist mimesis" which occurs with the rise of science and neoclassicism. On the other hand, in the era of modern double awareness, man or the self is still considered to remain unified, as Terry Eagleton says, "For some currents of postmodern thought, this subject [unified subject] would seem to have survived miraculously intact all the way from Christopher Marlowe to Iris

Murdoch" (34). At the same time it is perceived to be "dispersed, divided" (79), inconsistent and multiple owing to modern living on many levels. It is at this point that the parallel between the Shakespearian world and the modernist one breaks down. In the former, even if the background of either view of man is different, idealism or realism, the self has unity. But in the latter, the self is either unified or divided, reflecting the Newtonian mechanistic world view of the nineteenth century or the modern scientific revolution of Heisenberg's uncertainty principle. In other words, the self is considered to be either reality or illusion.

Though Shakespeare represents the self variously by way of disguise, it seems that Harold Pinter, who was a Shakespearian player in his youth, is influenced by the Shakespearian notions of disguise in the representation of the self in his plays. There are two kinds of disguise in Shakespearian disguise pattern. One is defined by M.C. Bradbrook as "the substitution, overlaying or metamorphosis of dramatic identity, whereby one character sustains two roles" ("Shakespeare" 160). The female page, such as Rosalind in *As You Like It* (1599-1600), sustains both a female and a male role by disguise, and becomes an ideal androgynously unified human being. The other type of disguise is suggested by Lloyd Davis: "The motif of disguise suggests that personal identity is not conceived as essentially or originally present" (4). The latter disguise is typically seen in Iago. He assumes "the disguise of the serpent," according to Bradbrook ("Shakespeare" 161). But his disguise shows he has no essential self as he says, "I am not what I am" (*Othello* [1604-05]1.1.66). In this type, each of two roles or two parts of the self produced by disguise is fictitious.

That disguise produces two roles or identities in a character implies that there is plurality or multiplicity in man. In humanist drama, this plurality reflects the ultimate One. In Pico della Mirandola's *Oration on The Dignity of Man*, God says to Adam, "thou mayest fashion thyself in whatever shape thou shalt prefer" (225). As Edgar Wind comments on this, all of the varied phases of this human self-transformation reflect "the ultimate One, of which they unfold particular aspects" (191). Accordingly, disguise produces a unified self with multiple elements. It reflects "the One behind the Many" (Giamatti 118). In *The Merchant of Venice* (1596-97), Portia, who disguises herself as a lawyer, Balthazar, becomes an ideal image of androgyny whose figure, the first and original man, Adam, takes as is seen in a neo-platonic interpretation of "Genesis i, 27: 'So God created man in his own image, in the image of God created he him; male and female created he them'" (Wind 212). Portia/Balthazar is an image of the ultimate One, too, in uniting Mercy and Justice which "are the contrary aspects of one deity: the God of vengeance is the God of love. His justice is mercy" (Wind 95).

But as is seen above, Pinter is one of the absurd dramatists whose works reflect the world of the "'new' modernity" (Baumer 402). This epistemological view of the world asserts the fictiveness or constructedness of the world. So in Pinter's works, a character has no unity of self, although Pinter makes his characters seem to have unified selves through realist representation. In creating his characters, Pinter uses "double awareness" and two kinds of disguise pattern.

As early as the 1960s John Russell Brown, a Shakespearian scholar, discerns the common interest between Pinter and Shakespeare regarding the self. Insisting that "Exposition has become Development, and Conclusion as well" in Pinter's plays, he says that *The Caretaker, A Slight Ache, The Dumb Waiter* and *The Collection* "progressively reveal the inner nature of their characters" ("Mr. Pinter's Shakespeare" 251). Though he admits "obvious differences between this 'Ancient' and the 'Moderns,'" saying that "Shakespeare never dispensed with a strong narrative Development," he recognizes "Shakespeare's progressive demonstration of character . . . within his fables" (258).

Double awareness and Shakespeare influenced Pinter as early as his school days at Hackney Downs in the 1940s, as Michael Billington points in an interview with Pinter ". . . *at school you gave a talk on realism and post-realism in French cinema*" (Pinter, "Harold" 74) and as Pinter mentions to Shakespeare: "Shakespeare dominated our lives at that time (I mean the lives of my friends and me)" (Pinter, "Speech" 71). This book attempts to explore the self in a selection of Pinter's plays from the perspective of the double awareness of modernism and of disguise in the shadow of Shakespeare.

1
Stanley's Ambiguous Self and Destiny: From the Modes of Representation and the Disguise Motif in *The Birthday Party*

About *The Birthday Party* (1957), Pinter's first full-length play, Marc Silverstein criticizes earlier critics such as Martin Esslin, Bernard F. Dukore, Steven H. Gale and Lois G. Gordon for discussing it "in terms of the tragic scenario (the autonomous self crushed by 'external force')" (*Harold Pinter* 28). For example, Gale says that "carried throughout *The Birthday Party* is the theme of the threat to a person's security by unknown outside powers and the disintegration of his individuality under the onslaught of the attacking force" (38). Against such "rhetoric of authenticity and the autonomous self" (*Harold Pinter* 47) Silverstein argues that the play dramatizes "the process through which the Other 'integrates' its subjects" (27). He sees in the play, "the formation, de-formation, and re-formation of Stanley's 'identity' " (*Harold Pinter* 26) in terms of the fictitiousness of the self. We might wonder, however, which view of the self and the hero's end fits the play best, in the oppositional views of both the autonomous self and the fictitious self, and the hero's disintegration and his integration (re-formation). When we try to discover the answer, we must first take into consideration the modes of representation in Pinter's plays, and second the disguise motif latent in the play.

The modern double awareness provides a hint to an answer as to Stanley's self and his destiny, and throws light on the ambiguity in each of them. At the same time Stanley's ambiguous self and destiny would be discernible also from the disguise motif in the play. It is well known that Pinter was in Anew McMaster's touring company when he was young, and played some roles in Shakespeare's plays which adopt 'disguise' parts.[1] As Pinter made an appearance in *As You Like It* and *Othello*, he would have known the two kinds of disguise which we saw in the introduction.

From the fact that Stanley Webber has another name, "Joe Soap" (60), the perspective of the disguise motif, too, would clarify what Stanley's self and his destiny are like. Focusing on the theme of the play as the individual versus an external power such as the Establishment or some organization, we can investigate how Stanley's self and his end are developed.

1

When we see *The Birthday Party* in the mode of realism, we notice that the play dramatizes the process through which external power threatens an individualist, and transforms him into a man who conforms to the external power or the Establishment, whether such transformation means his death or rebirth. Stanley, who is a pianist with "a unique touch" (32), can be considered an individualist who makes much of the individual's autonomy rather than conformity to society. So he finds peaceful seclusion in Meg's boarding house in a seaside resort after his bitter experience of the people's humiliation of him following "a great success" (32) at Lower Edmonton. He explains to Meg the people's great admiration and betrayal of the genius on piano as follows:

> I had a unique touch. Absolutely unique. They came up to me. They came up to me and said they were grateful. Champagne we had that night, the lot. . . . Yes. Lower Edmonton. Then after that, you know

what they did? They carved me up. . . . My next concert. . . . I went down there to play. Then, when I got there, the hall was closed, the place was shuttered up, not even a caretaker. They'd locked it up. (32-33)

Meg sympathizes with such an alienated individualist ("You stay here. You'll be better off. You stay with your old Meg" [33]), and though she tries to establish a mother-son-lover relation between her and Stanley, Stanley doesn't submit to her ruling him, but rather stirs up his sense of autonomy. When she takes away his tea before his drinking and makes an excuse for his complaint ("You didn't want it!" [31]), he says decisively,

> Who said I didn't want it!
> . . . .
> Who gave you the right to take away my tea?
> . . . .
> Tell me, Mrs Boles, when you address yourself to me, do you ever ask yourself who exactly you are talking to? Eh? (31)

This episode illustrates how he is very conscious of his independent self and identity. There is no doubt that this 'self' in him derives from "the autonomous, unified self-generating subject postulated by essentialist humanism" (Dollimore 155) which emerges "in the latter part of the seventeenth century and the eighteenth century" (Dollimore 156). Such an autonomous self or "the unified subject of liberal humanism" (Belsey 33), when he is an artist, is a further "threat to the status quo because it [piano playing] is not a thing that everyone can do equally well and because it requires a different set of goals from those held by the ordinary workingman" (Gale 55).

It is Goldberg and McCann who confront such an antisocial independent man. Though their identities are ambiguous, we can surmise that they are representatives of some external power. When Stanley knows of their coming to the boarding house earlier, he at once feels a threat and is afraid of the Other searching for him and invading his 'self.' He asks Meg repeatedly, "Who are they?" (30) and declares, "They're looking for someone. A certain person" (34), being convinced that he is the target. His forecast that "They've got a wheelbarrow in that van" (34) proves to be true later ("What would Mr Goldberg want with a wheelbarrow?" [79]).

Stanley who is anxious to know their identities and their purpose attempts to spy into their truths by using disguise, much like Hamlet who disguises himself as a mad man to spy on Claudius and his followers.[2] Maintaining the essential autonomous self, he assumes another false identity. Stanley, who knows one of the visitors has a Irish name, McCann ("My name's McCann" [47]), disguises himself as a sociable man and tries to invite McCann to an Irish pub ("I know Ireland very well. I've many friends there. . . . What about coming out to have a drink with me? There's a pub down the road serves draught Guinness" [52]). To Goldberg Stanley disguises himself as another different man. He assumes the role of the manager of the boarding house, lying to him, "I run the house. I'm afraid you and your friend will have to find other accommodation" (54). He tries to banish them out of the house for the reason that "We're booked out. Your room is taken" (54). Although he continues his extempore disguise toward them, he keeps his original self as he says, "I suppose I have changed, but I'm still the same man that I always was" (50).

But Goldberg is more skillful than Stanley in using disguise. Following Esslin's argument that *The Birthday Party* is "a kind of modern *Everyman*" (*Peopled Wound* 82), Elin Diamond argues that Goldberg is one of the descendants of "the Vice of the fifteenth- and sixteenth-century morality plays" (45):

> ... we can ... recognize him [the Vice] in characters as diverse as Diccon, "the bedlam," of Mr. S.'s *Gammer Gurton's Needle*, Iago of Shakespeare's *Othello*, and Goldberg in Pinter's *The Birthday Party*. All three exhibit the Vice's clever scheming, his dissembling, his gulling of simple characters ... his motiveless malice. (47)

Iago, who is referred to as an heir of the Vice, is typical of the disguise of the serpent, one of the two archetypes of disguise, which originates with the Vice. M.C. Bradbrook says,

> The two archtypes were the disguise of the serpent and the disguise of the Incarnation. The devil's power of deceit furnished plots for many moralities. In Medwall's *Nature*, in *Respublica* and in Skelton's *Magnifycence*, the vices take the virtues' names. ... There is no direct disguise in ... Iago ... but an assumed personality.
> ("Shakespeare" 161)[3]

Considering these arguments and Goldberg's plural names ("Nat," "Simey" [53],"Benny" [88]),[4] it is probable that Goldberg disguises himself as a businessman with "a brief case" (36), hiding his real identity as someone who seems to be a representative or an instrument of the external power or the Establishment. His main purpose for visiting Stanley is finally to force him to conform to some "external force" (60) or society among whose members he is.

To promote his aim, Goldberg makes use of Stanley's birthday which Meg informed him of, proposing to hold a party. The strategy which he uses in ruling and transforming Stanley is very cunning, like Iago. Firstly, he disturbs the autonomous unified self in him, disorients it, and breaks it down, just as Iago sways Othello's strong belief in Desdemona's chastity, cracks and destroys it. Secondly, he forces Stanley to assume a new self or identity which conforms to "an external force" whose follower he is ("Do you recognise an external force, responsible for you, suffering for you?" [60]).

2

Before the birthday party, Goldberg and McCann interrogate Stanley severely to sway his unified self, and disorient it. First, Goldberg asks him, "what were you doing yesterday?" "And the day before. What did you do the day before that?" (57), and disturbs his sense of time. To the perplexed Stanley's question "What do you mean?" Goldberg thrusts on him the identity of a social "washout" who is "wasting everybody's time" (57), substituting it for his native self. And Goldberg starts to destroy his sense of identity, saying falsely, one after another, "Why are you driving that old lady off her conk?" "Why do you force that old man out to play chess?" "Why do you treat that young lady like a leper?" (57), contrary to Stanley's friendly relation to Meg, Petey and Lulu. Goldberg is fabricating multiple Stanleys to disintegrate his unified autonomous self, and force him to assume a fictitious identity which he presses on him. While he is made a traitor to his organization ("Why did you leave the organization?" "Why did you betray us?" [58]), he is thrown into a variety of identities or roles, such as social, sexual and religious criminal or sinner. He is accused of killing his wife ("Why did you kill your wife?" [59]), of raping his mother ("Mother defiler!" [61]), and of discarding his belief ("When did you last pray?" [60], "You're a traitor to the cloth" [61]). But some of his and McCann's questionings are incoherent and haphazard. Goldberg asks inconsistently, "Why did you never get married?" after his question "How did you kill her?" (59). Further, they continue to ask unanswerable questions, "Is the number 846 possible or necessary?" (60). To Stanley's answer "Neither," Goldberg says "Wrong!" and asks it again. Though Stanley answers "Both" this time, these hit-or-miss replies of his would show the disorientation of his mind. And when Goldberg asks him "Why did the chicken cross the road?" (61) and McCann asks "Chicken? Egg? Which came first?" (62), Stanley, at last, "*screams*" (62) and reveals his mind's collapse. Their persistent inquisition, which attempts to disorient Stanley, has resulted in disintegrating his original unified self. Seeing his disruption, McCann asks him, "Who are you, Webber?" (62) while Goldberg declares him dead ("You're dead" [62]). As if corresponding to Goldberg saying, "There's no juice in you" (62), Stanley does nothing but groan and repeat "Uuuuuhhhh!" (62). The wordless Stanley seems to have lost his autonomous, and humanist self, lacking reason. Gale argues about the inquisition scene,

> The confrontation scene is the crux of the play. . . . it is not a particular which is important; since there is no way to escape the all-encompassing catalogue, the stress is on the idea of inevitability which ultimately defeats Stanley. (53)

Though Gale contends that "the party might better be described as a wake celebrating the death of Stan as an individual" (53), Stanley is 'resurrected' in Act III. In the second confrontation scene, Goldberg uses disguise again to 'resurrect' him. His way of manipulating disguise is similar to Petruchio's strategy in *The Taming of the Shrew* (1593-94). When Petruchio tries to tame Kate, his stratagem is to thrust a hypothetical modest identity on her, and change identities. It is to force the rude Kate to assume a kind of Griselda-self from the outside. So Petruchio calls her "passing gentle" (2.1.236) or "sweet Katherine" (2.1.260), despite her anger ("Go, fool, and whom thou keep'st command" 2.1.251).

> PETRUCHIO. 'Twas told me you were rough, and coy, and sullen,
> And now I find report a very liar;
> For thou are pleasant, gamesome, passing courteous,
> But slow in speech, yet sweet as spring-time flowers.
> (2.1.237-40)

What Petruchio aims to do here is to transform her into a woman who conforms to the Establishment. The ideal woman who fits most in contemporary patriarchy is a modest, silent and obedient woman whom St. Paul shows in Ephesians (5. 22), and 1 Timothy (2. 9-12). It is a hypothetical identity thrust on the shrewish Kate by Petruchio.

Goldberg adopts the same strategy as Petruchio to the broken-down Stanley. When the disintegrated Stanley appears the next day after the party to be taken away to Monty, it is "STANLEY, *who is dressed in a dark well cut suit and white collar*" (91) that we encounter. As Silverstein points out Stanley's appearance is "the uniform of the conservative English businessman" (47). Stanley is, at the end, made Goldberg's copy. In the first edition of the play, Stanley wears striped trousers and a black jacket, and carries a bowler hat:

> *He [McCann] ushers in STANLEY, who is dressed in striped trousers, black jacket, and white collar. He carries a bowler hat in one hand....* (53)

Such an appearance suggests his funeral. "The revised edition," on the contrary, Charles A. Carpenter argues, "changes Stanley's image into a duplicate of Goldberg's" (400), resurrecting him as a conformist who wears a dark suit.

> *He ushers in STANLEY, who is dressed in a dark well cut suit and white collar. He holds his broken glasses in his hand.* (91)

So, in the second inquisition scene after his appearance, Goldberg and McCann force him to assume a socially conformist self.

> GOLDBERG. From now on, we'll be the hub of your wheel.
> MCCANN. We'll renew your season ticket.
> GOLDBERG. We'll take tuppence off your morning tea.
> MCCANN. We'll give you a discount on all inflammable goods.
> GOLDBERG. We'll watch over you.
> MCCANN. Advise you.
> GOLDBERG. Give you proper care and treatment.
> MCCANN. Let you use the club bar.
> GOLDBERG. Keep a table reserved. (92-93)

As they say, "You'll be re-orientated," "You'll be adjusted" (93), and "You'll be integrated" (94), Stanley is forced to assume such social identities as "success" (93), "magnate," "statesman" (94), a different socially conformed self from the original autonomous and independent one. It goes without saying that such a "new man" (91) is a puppet manipulated by the status quo or its obedient instrument. This is confirmed by Stanley's remaining silent up to the end except emitting "sounds from the throat"

("Uh-gug . . . uh-gug. . . eeehhh-gag . . . Caahh . . . caahh," [94]), though Goldberg pretends to take care of him, saying to Petey, "We're taking him to Monty" (95), because he suffered a "Nervous breakdown" (81) at the party. In this reading, Stanley is, as it were, dead as an individual, even if he is to be socially "integrated." Gale agrees to this destiny of Stanley: "He has been reduced to the level of a cipher—a nonthinking, nonreacting member of a smoothly running mechanistic society in his neat, conservative dress . . ." (54-55).

3

Monty's institution seems to be not a hospital but a place where Stanley is transformed substantially into a hypothetical conformist self which Goldberg thrust him on by way of disguise. Robert Gordon refers to it as "a state mental sanitarium of the kind used by totalitarian governments to carry out behavior modification treatment on dissidents" (42). Monty's institution might have a Nazi background. As Goldberg says to Stanley, "You'll be integrated" (94), which means his forced assuming of a new conformist self, the word "integration" suggests the forced conformity to the Nazi regime. According to Charles Grimes,

> Goldberg says "You'll be integrated" (84), reusing a word featured in Nazi oppression against those people (not only Jews) deemed antisocial who needed to be "integrated" back into productive society. . . . The process by which the Nazis came to regulate and coordinate all dimensions of human activity (political, social, economic, philosophical, artistic, legal) in accordance with Hitler's vision was called *Gleichschaltung*, literally "parallel switching," often translated as "integration." This system of forced conformity symbolizes in Pinter's political imagination the violent depersonal-

ization of which society is always capable. (41-42)

Whether Goldberg and McCann are agents of the Gestapo or not, their aim is certainly to depersonalize Stanley or rob of him the autonomous liberal self, and install conformist one instead. But do they succeed in it completely?

Petey, who feels Stanley's danger in his being taken to Monty, risks stopping their abduction of him ("Leave him alone!" 95). But, being threatened with his own abduction ("Come with us to Monty. There's plenty of room in the car" [96]), he shouts, "Stan, don't let them tell you what to do!" (96). He encourages him neither to lose his own autonomous self, nor to submit to their despotic vision. He is sure that such an original liberal self remains in him, even if he cannot utter the words at all.

His conviction of it would be backed up by the voiceless Stanley's sporadic physical resistance to them. We can witness such violence of resistance in his kicking Goldberg after the first inquisition in Act II.

> GOLDBERG. . . . There's no juice in you. You're nothing but an odour!
> *Silence. . . . He is crouched in the chair. He looks up slowly and kicks GOLDBERG in the stomach.* (62)

The greatest bodily defiance would be Stanley's defecating in front of them. At the end of the second inquisition in which Stanley's "integration" is foretold, Goldberg and McCann ask him again and again about this future, "What's your opinion, sir? Of this prospect, sir?" (94) or " What do you say, Stan?" (95). Stage directions, during their persistent repetition of the question, show his bodily motions as follows:

> *He draws a long breath which shudders down his body. He concentrates.*
>
> . . . .
>
> *His head lowers, his chin draws into his chest, he crouches.*
>
> . . . .
>
> STANLEY's *body shudders, relaxes, his head drops, he becomes still again, stooped.* (94-95)

Carpenter construes the sequence of these movements on his part as "the motions of defecating, baby fashion" (400), and asserts that "Stanley's profanity is his last rebellious gesture" (400). Furthermore, as for "Caahh . . . caahh" (95) voiced by Stanley, Carpenter points out that "In many countries, 'caca' (from the Greek root kakka-) is 'shit' in little boy's language" (400). Stanley is insulting them here. Pinter admits later that Petey's line to Stanley is one of resistance, saying to Mel Gussow, "Petey says, 'Stan, don't let them tell you what to do.' I've lived that line all my damn life" (Gussow 71). Pinter himself was an unyielding activist late in his life, as is well known.[5]

Although Stanley shows physically that the autonomous self is still existent in him, there is much probability that he is to be transformed into a conformist subject submissive to the Establishment, whether it is the system of totalitarianism like the Nazi regime, or that of "the reified, bureaucratized order of advanced capitalism" (Silverstein, *Harold Pinter* 47). After all, in the context of realism, it can be affirmed, that Pinter displays the ambiguity of Stanley's self and his destiny.

4

Malcolm Bradbury and James McFarlane argue that "Modernism" is "the art consequent on Heisenberg's 'Uncertainty principle' "and say further,

It is the art consequent on the dis-establishing of . . . conventional notions of causality, on the destruction of traditional notions of the wholeness of individual character, on the linguistic chaos that ensues . . . when all realities have become subjective fictions. (27)

As mentioned earlier, this play has a view of double awareness, and crosses "a spectrum of realism and modernism." So seeing it from the viewpoint of modernism, we are aware of some devices in it by which we suspect that realities can be reduced to fictions. Up to the moment when two visitors appear, we perceive domestic realism in the dialogues between three persons in the seaside boardinghouse and the action of the play, which center on a pseudo mother-son-lover relation between Meg and Stanley. The conversation starts between Meg and her husband Petey about his breakfast ("MEG. Here's your cornflakes. . . . Are they nice? / PETEY. Very nice" [19]), and the newspaper he is reading ("What are you reading?" / "Someone's just had a baby" [21]), and when Meg asks, "Is Stanley up yet?" (20), the action develops toward the relation between her and Stanley. Meg, who goes upstairs to fetch him, calls him "Stan! Stanny!" in a term of endearment (23), mothering him; when Stanley enters the living-room and criticizes the fried bread as "Succulent" (27) in a tone of sarcasm, she interprets the word sexually ("You shouldn't say that word to a married woman" [27]), betraying her love to him.

But with the appearance of Goldberg and McCann, Ronald Knowles says that "theatricality compromises realism" (32) because "a version of the music hall cross-talk act is introduced, with Goldberg as the articulate, outlandish stage Jew and McCann the mournful Irish stooge" (32).

MCCANN. Is this it?
GOLDBERG. This is it.
MCCANN. Are you sure?
GOLDBERG. Sure I'm sure. (37)

As in *The Dumb Waiter* (1957), gangster movie echoes are also heard in the two visitors, who seem to be hit men whose aim is to pursue and kill Stanley, a target. Such a sudden mixing of other genres, comedy or thriller, in the context of realism may be considered as the Brechtian effect of alienation (*Verfremdungseffect*), which reduces reality to illusion or fiction. This insight from modernism leads us to doubt the existence of the autonomous unified self in Stanley. Is a supreme pianist, Stanley, with a unique touch, genuine?

It is well known that modernist writers wrote of "a vanishing self, an incoherent self, a decentralized self, of a self that possibly did not even exist" (Baumer 420). Man is not considered as a unified person but as "a concatenation of split units" (Behera 51). When we see Stanley in this modernist view, we suspect that the image of himself as an "absolute unique" pianist (32) might be not essential but fictitious. Silverstein considers it as something like an illusion reflected in the mirror stage of Lacan:

> . . . the "self," rather than some core of being inhering within the subject, issues from the Other. If we ask what defines Stanley's identity as pianist, the answer is not his "unique touch," but the Other, whose gaze and actions become a mirror in which Stanley sees reflected his "essence": (*Harold Pinter* 29)

In Stanley's case, the Other is the audience of his concert at Lower

Edmonton. Stanley narrates to Meg his remembrance of it: "I had a unique touch. Absolutely unique. They came up to me. They came up to me and said they were grateful" (32-33). The self from the Other or the fictitious self in Stanley may be called the alienation of the subject because "Stanley's definition of identity in terms of an (illusory) 'absolutely unique' essence confines him in 'the armour of an alienating identity,'[6] alienating to the extent that it grounds itself in an image and bars him from perceiving his truth" (Silverstein, *Harold Pinter* 30).

Whether Stanley's original self is the self issuing from the Other or the alienated one, it has the possibility of fictitiousness. If so, the kind of disguise which is related to him in the play proves to be like Lloyd Davis's definition, according to which disguise suggests that "personal identity is not conceived as essentially or originally present" (4). Though he uses disguise in spying on Goldberg and McCann as seen above, each of the two selves or identities produced by disguise turns illusory. The absolutely unique pianist as inherent self is also fictitious at the same time as his assumed self as the sociable man or manager of the house is illusory.

This argument urges us to infer that Stanley's disguise itself is a symbol of the fictitiousness of his whole self. If so, his narrative of the piano concert might be a lie. As Robert Gordon says "he appears to be pretending to Meg that he has been offered a world tour as a concert pianist" (33). His narrative has the possibility of being a red herring to avoid the topic of the two visitors. For Stanley has a chance to run away from the authorities, disguising himself as a pianist. Knowles puts a contemporary topical event behind this possibility. According to Knowles, Irish Republican Army (IRA) activity was prevalent in England after the war. Its leader "John Stephenson" used the assumed name "Sean Stephenson" and other aliases (36); in other words he used disguise.

Knowles argues about its influence on Stanley: "Pinter wrote the play in 1957 with Stanley in mind as having arrived sometime in 1955-56, directly in the aftermath of the Arborfield raid when many IRA men were known to have fled" (37). Stanley, too, has the alias of Joe Soap. When Goldberg asks him, "Why did you change your name? and "What's your name now?" he answers, "Joe Soap" (60). He might have fled and lied hidden in Meg's house, and been discovered by the agents. Anyway Stanley's self is judged to be ambiguous.

5

Both Goldberg's and McCann's identities are ambiguous. While they seem to be the realistic agents of the authorities who pursue Stanley, these threatening strangers are "also coded as stock comedic gangsters, Jewish and Irish" as Begley says (42). Their representation as types would substantiate an idea of the self as construct or fiction. They also might reflect the modernist idea of the self.

Besides such an aspect, Goldberg and McCann might have another phase as doubles of Stanley. Knowles points this out, saying that " . . . Pinter's poem of 1958, 'A view of the Party,' offers an expressionist perspective—'The thought that Goldberg was / Sat in the center of the room'[7]—as if the intruders are objectifications of Stanley's mind" (33). Not only Knowles but also Lois G. Gordon regards them as the projections of Stanley's interior. Admitting the complexity of their function, she contends that "they are less external forces—satanic messengers from the void or malign universe—than projections of Stanley's guilt, driving and uncompromising internal furies" (27). Although she recognizes their function as projections of Stanley's mind from the viewpoint of Stanley as the Oedipal son, we see them as the doubles of Stanley's self or the parts of his broken self from the modernist viewpoint. In modernism, Esslin argues that "Expressionist drama is full of *Doppelgänger* figures, characters which are merely aspects of the hero's personality which have split off and have taken on an independent existence . . ." (" Modernist" 534).

Let's look at the examples. The first inquisition scene dramatizes what the disintegration of Stanley's self is like, and displays a completely fractured self at the end in the form of its screaming with inarticulate words. And then the succeeding party scene reflects the externalization of the split self in Goldberg and McCann. There Goldberg seduces Lulu sexually ("Lulu, you're a big bouncy girl. Come and sit on my lap" [68]) and she accepts ("I've always liked older men" [70]). But in the context of modernism or expressionism, the sexual Goldberg is considered to reflect the voluptuary part of Stanley's self as his double. For the lustful element has been lurking in Stanley. When Lulu allures him to go outside ("Come out and get a bit of air. . . ." [36]) in Act I, he first agrees to it ("How would you like to go away with me?"), but finally refuses it ("I can't at the moment") to her scorn ("You're a bit of a washout, aren't you?" [36]). But later, at end of the party, Stanley's lust gushes out suddenly when he attacks her, and tries to rape her triumphantly: "LULU *is lying spread-eagled on the table,* STANLEY *bent over her.* STANLEY, *as soon as the torchlight hits him, begins to giggle*" (75).

As for the other double, McCann, he is liable to be violent. The tendency is discernible early in his irritation at Stanley and his order to him ("Mind it. Leave it" [49]) when Stanley casually "*picks up a strip of paper*" (49), which McCann tore from a sheet of newspaper. We also witness, in the party scene, the eruption of his violence when he "*breaks* STANLEY'S *glasses, snapping the frames*" (73), and "*picks up the drum and places it sideways in* STANLEY'S *path*" so that he "*falls over with his foot caught in it*" (73). The drum which put Stanley into danger symbolizes Stanley's tendency of violence, too. Stanley, when he is given the drum as a birthday present by Meg, beats it in return before her. At first he is beating it regularly, but gradually his beating becomes more and more "*erratic, uncontrolled,*" he "*banging the drum, his face and the drumbeat savage and possessed*" to Meg's "*dismay*" (46). This savage way of his beating the drum suggests the latency of violence in him. Through the drum McCann also turns out to be the double of Stanley. For the end of the party unfolds Stanley's violence in his strangling Meg with his foot thrust into the drum: "*He begins to move towards* MEG, *dragging the drum on his foot. . . . His hands move towards her and they reach her throat. He begins to strangle her*" (73-74).

6

In the context of this modernist reading—the self's issuing from the Other, Stanley's assumption of disguise and the existence of his doubles—Stanley's self has proved to be by the end of his birthday party disintegrated and therefore fictitious. If so, in this perspective, how can we see the end or destiny of Stanley when he wears a dark well-cut suit and white collar to be taken to Monty?

Though Silverstein recognizes Stanley's integration or re-formation represented by his clothing, that self doesn't mean an autonomous unified one, but the constructed or fictitious self. His rebirth means "his assumption of an identity created by and *in the image of* the omnipotent Other" (*Harold Pinter* 35). "In the mirror of Goldberg and McCann's language," Silverstein contends, "Stanley will see his subjectivity 'through the eyes of the other,' through the Other's codes and categories of evaluation" (*Harold Pinter* 37): his integration is the "integration within the reified, bureaucratized order of advanced capitalism" (*Harold Pinter* 47). Goldberg functions not only as Stanley's double but also as the Other in the play.

Advanced capitalism can also be called "late capitalism" (Jameson 412) in which we find "the so-called death of the subject, or, more exactly, the fragmented and schizophrenic decentering and dispersion of this last" (Jameson 413). As mentioned above, the first edition of the play shows the dead Stanley with funeral clothes on. The modernist reading would recognize this schizophrenic dispersion of self in the fictitiously integrated Stanley at the end. And the reading would tell us that the world where this self lives is existentially absurd. Though Dobretz contends about Len in *The Dwarfs* (1960) that "The Other is able to enter Len at will . . . to deprive him of his kingdom, of his room, of his identity, to reduce him to the state of schizophrenia or loss of Self . . . " (320), the same is true of Stanley. The Other, or Goldberg, invades his self, destroys it, and reduces it to schizophrenia, although Goldberg describes Stanley's final mental condition as a "Nervous breakdown" (81).

Goldberg as the Other is a kind of symbol of the world, too, since he is an agent of the external power or the world. The world surrounding Stanley robs him of words and meaning. It is a world like that of *Macbeth* (1605-06), in which a tale is "Told by an idiot (schizophrenia), full of sound and fury ('U h-gug . . . hehhh-gag . . . Cahhh . . .' [94]), / Signifying nothing" (5. 5. 26-28). The meaningless and absurd world is threatening to an individual, and makes man feel anxious and alienated because there are no more absolutes like God. Stanley is alienated from all people, except Petey after the arrival of the two visitors. Meg, at first, seems to take care of him as a surrogate mother, but she does no more than live in her own self-delusion selfishly, which results in her self-conceit as "the belle of the ball" (97) even after the party. Since Stanley's birthday party was proposed by Goldberg, her interest has moved completely from Stanley to her party dress ("I'll put on my party dress" [43], "You like my dress?" [63]), or the visitors' praises and flatteries to her ("Madam, you'll look like a tulip" [43], "Beautiful! A beautiful speech. . . . That was a lovely toast" [65]). Alienating Stanley during the party, she is attracted to McCann ("Oh, what a lovely voice" [70]), and being absorbed in her own fantasy world of the past ("My little room was pink. I had a pink carpet and pink curtains, and I had musical boxes all over the room . . ." [70]).

Ironically it is not only Stanley but also Goldberg who lives in the same waste land. Whereas Goldberg, in destroying Stanley, seems to show an impersonal phase as only an instrument of external power, he also reveals a contrary personal aspect, his self's disintegration or impasse, feeling depressed and alienated like Stanley. Just before he takes Stanley to Monty, he says suddenly, "I don't know why, but I feel knocked out. I feel a bit . . . It's uncommon for me" (86). It is because he has recognized the absurdity of the world.

>   GOLDBERG. . . . . . .
>   Because I believe that the world . . . (*Vacant.*) . . . .
>   Because I believe that the world . . . (*Desperate.*) . . . .
>   Because I BELIEVE THAT THE WORLD . . . (*Lost.*) . . . . (88)

Goldberg says earlier that "We all wander on our tod through this world. It's a lonely pillow to kip on" (66).

This sudden "Nervous breakdown" (81) of his, which he himself ascribes to Stanley as his symptom earlier, impresses on us that the drama foretells the same destiny of Goldberg and Stanley. His being the double of Stanley implies this, too. In the age of absurd late capitalism, a man is destined to be "knocked out" and reduced to schizophrenia, and thereafter he is taken to Monty so that he may be a new submissive instrument of the external power or the world. The world in the twentieth century is one produced subjectively and cruelly. Husserl and Heidegger argue that the world is reconstructed by the human mind or consciousness while an absurdist, Esslin says, "the twentieth century world is one of organized cruelty on a large scale" ("Harold Pinter's Theatre" 30). If the cruel world is reconstructed subjectively, the victimizer can be a victim in turn. This possibility for Goldberg will be illuminated in the last scene of *The Dumb Waiter*.[8]

Thus in the modernist context *The Birthday Party* shows the self's fictitiousness, and the miserable state of an individual's destiny. But as the context of realism implies the possibility of the autonomous self and the hero's resistance, too, it can be concluded that the play as a whole does not negate completely "a human subject unified enough to embark on significantly transformative action" (Eagleton 16), only confirming "the schizoid, disheveled subject" (Eagleton 16) and his destruction, but displays the ambiguity of the self and his destiny. This could be what Pinter argued about this play in his Nobel lecture, "Art, Truth, and Politics " (2005): "In my play *The Birthday Party* I think I allow a whole range of options to operate in a dense forest of possibility before finally focusing on an act of subjugation" ("Art, Truth" 287-88).

The possibility of Stanley's resistance to the establishment, even if it is doubtful, will be realized in Luth's opposition to Lenny and Max through disguise in *The Homecoming* (1964).

Notes
1. In 1951, 1952 and 1953, Pinter played Charles the Wrestler in *As You Like It*, Horatio in *Hamlet*, Edgar and Edmund in *King Lear*, Cassio and Iago in *Othello*, Bassanio in *The Merchant of Venice*, Hortensio in *The Taming of the Shrew*. Cf. Thompson 127-78
2. Hamlet, who heard from his father's ghost of his murder by Claudius, decides to "put an antic disposition on" (*Hamlet* 1.5.180) so that he may spy on Claudius and confirm the ghost's disclosure. M.C. Bradbrook includes

Hamlet's pretending to be a madman in disguise: "Disguise ranges from the simple fun of the quick-change artist . . . to the antic disposition of Edgar or Hamlet. . . . it may be better translated for the modern age by such terms as 'alternating personality'" ("Shakespeare" 160).

3. In *Magnifycence*, "Counterfeit Countenance becomes Good Demeanance, Crafty Conveyance becomes Sure Surveyance, Courtly Abusion becomes Lusty Pleasure and Cloaked Collusion becomes Sober Sadness" (Bradbrook, "Shakespeare" 161). In the list of "The partes and names of the plaiers" of *Respublica*, "Avarice" is written as "allias policie the vice of the plaie" (Udal, *Respublica* 1).

4. Goldberg says that his mother and wife called him "Simey" (53, 69) while "My father said to me, Benny, Benny . . ." (88). As McCann says to his surprise, "I thought your name was Nat" (53), Nat might be an assumed name which is used when he works. For the name of Nat derives from Natham. Bernard F. Dukore argues that

> As Natham the prophet, commanded directly by God, rebuked King David for having sinned against the Lord, and brought him back to the paths of righteousness, so does Nat, commanded directly by his organization, bring Stanley back to the paths of conformity. ("Theatre" 52)

Goldberg, who assumes "the disguise of the serpent," might have an alias unlike Iago, but like the vices in *Magnifycence*.

5. Pinter continued to attack US foreign policy described as 'low intensity conflict' in which

> thousands of people die but slower than if you dropped a bomb on them in one fell swoop. It means that you infect the heart of the country, that you establish a malignant growth and watch the gangrene bloom. When the populace has been subdued . . . and your own friends, the military and the great corporations, sit comfortably in power, you go before the camera and say that democracy has prevailed. ("Art, Truth" 289-90)

6. The original note number of this quotation is 11, whose quotation is from Jacques Lacan, *Écrits: A Selection*, trans. By Alan Sheridan (New York: W. W. Norton, 1977), 2.

7. The original note number of this quotation is 9, whose quotation is from

Collected Poems and Prose (London: Faber, 1991), 46.

8. The two killers, Ben and Gus, are waiting for instructions about the next target from their boss, Wilson, in some basement room. Wilson, who doesn't appear on the stage at all, symbolizes some external power while the two men represent its instruments. After Gus with the revolver in its holster goes out to drink water, Ben receives an unidentified order through the tube, and replies "Sure we're ready" (164). When the *"door right opens sharply,"* and Ben *"turns, his revolver levelled at the door,"* it is Gus *"stripped of . . . revolver"* (165) who appears. *"They stare at each other"* (165), and the curtain falls. This final symmetrical tableau shows that a victimizer Ben will become a victim someday, because in the play the "two appear halves of the whole rather than separate . . . coherent entities" (88), as Begley says.

2
Davies's Disguise in *The Caretaker*: From the Views of Modernist Negation and the Tradition of Disguise

When an old tramp in Pinter's *The Caretaker* (1959), whose "real name" is "Mac Davies," is brought to Aston's room and says, "I been going around under the assumed name," "Bernard Jenkins" (29), we know that he has two identities, and now is disguising himself as Jenkins. His case is considered to be the overlaying of dramatic identity in M.C. Bradbrook's definition of disguise as "the substitution, overlaying or metamorphosis of dramatic identity, whereby one character sustains two roles" ("Shakespeare" 160). Seemingly it is a little difficult for us to distinguish Davies's and Jenkins's roles, but as it is true that the tramp at the outset of the play is conscious of his past self ("I've eaten my dinner off the best of plates" [18]) and his present one ("I might have been on the road a few years" [18]), we may argue that he has two selves, and that the disguise, which the change of name shows, confirms it. If so, we wonder what his real self (Davies) and his assumed one (Jenkins) are really like. This chapter attempts to illuminate these two selves and how Davies's disguise, which produces the two selves, works in relation to the views of modernism and the tradition of disguise.

1

Because Davies so often asserts that "my papers" at Sidcup "prove who I am" (28, 29), and because his main concern through the drama is to go there to collect them, so that he can "prove everything" (29), and "be fixed up" (25) without roving anymore, there would be no doubt that this tramp has a real identity or self besides his assumed one. And when we look for some outstanding features of his which tell the actual state of it, from his rambling speeches, we take note of his self-assertion and self-respect first of all. When Davies is offered a cigarette by Aston, he refuses it and, instead, he asserts that "I'll have a bit of that tobacco there for my pipe, if you like" because "It was knocked off on the Great West Road" (17). He asserts himself cogently based on cause and effect principles. His self-esteem is shown when "the guvnor give me the bullet" for the unjust reason of his making "too much commotion": "I told him that. . . . nobody's got more rights than I have. Let's have a bit of fair play" (19). His words betray his consciousness of his position as "Promethean man" in spite of his appearance as a shabby tramp. It was the people's "treating me like dirt" (17) and imposing an unreasonable and extra job on him that caused him to complain at his workplace:

> DAVIES. Comes up to me, parks a bucket of rubbish at me tells me to take it out the back. It's not my job to take out the bucket! They got a boy there for taking out the bucket. . . . My job's cleaning the floor . . . doing a bit of washing-up. . . . (18)

Though he "might have been on the road" (19), he is proud of having been a human being or bourgeois ("I've had a dinner with the best" [18]). Judging from these speeches, he is much like a traditional man who "had some idea how to talk to old people with the proper respect," and "was brought up with the right ideas" (19).

That is the reason why he gets angry, being treated as a dog or wild animal when he went to the monastery at Luton where he expected a pair of shoes would be given, but "Piss off" (23) was their reply with only a meal as small as a bird could eat being served: "Meal they give me! A bird . . . a little tiny bird, he could have ate it in under two minutes. Right, they said to me, you've had your meal, get off out of it. Meal? I said, what do you think I am, a dog? Nothing better than a dog. What do you think I am, a wild animal ?" (23-24).

These anecdotes of inhumane treatment and his angry response to them induce us to suppose that Davies's self is the "liberal humanist self" (Eagleton 91), which was pervasive from the Enlightenment through the nineteenth century when the view of the world became a mechanistic Newtonian one. The figure of this man is called "Rational Man and Promethean Man" (Baumer 87). But this traditional self which was cultivated mainly by the Enlightenment thought had ironically a possibility of embracing barbarism because "implicit in the beginning of the Enlightenment, in Rousseau, Kant, and Hegel, was the synthesis of reason, domination, and myth that was . . . put into practice in Auschwitz" (Herf 233-34). Its phase of barbarism seems to be projected on his hostility to aliens such as "Poles, Greeks, Blacks" (17). That he has such a 'humanist self' is clear in his antithetical behavior in which whereas he persists in his white Britishness ("fair's fair" [27], "I was! [born and bred in the British isles] " [42]), he emphasizes Blacks' dirtiness ("Blacks . . . using the lavatory. . . . it was all dirty in there" [68]).

Even if a 'liberal humanist self,' which the first identity Davies represents is problematic, its essential presence in him can be glimpsed from a reading of realism as above. But should we think that all of Davies's speeches are true and trustworthy, following only a mode of reading based on realism? As Pinter himself says, "there can be no hard distinctions between what is real and what is unreal, nor between what is true and what is false" ("Writing for the Theatre" 11). He can be regarded as a modernist whose awareness is double. He sees the world both objectively and subjectively.

From another similar viewpoint of modernism (especially high modernism), a principle of modernist negation, Varun Begley says in his analysis of *The Caretaker*, "Both plays [*The Birthday Party* and *The Caretaker*] might be described as quasi-realism, though I would argue that *The Caretaker* . . . negates the realities it intermittently signals," based on "a principle of modernist negation that encourages and then complicates social interpretation" (48). He suggests that the inhuman monastery anecdote might be Davies's fiction, not truth:

> The army of incongruities arrayed against interpretation is led by the monk who tells Davies to 'piss off out of it.' 'If you don't piss off,' he reportedly says, 'I'll kick you all the way to the gate.' The inappropriateness (to say the least) of this response, its clipped, skeptical diction, posits an elemental doubt about the *value* of the anecdote . . . . (62)

From modernist negation, Begley implies the fictiveness of Aston's anecdote of electroshock treatment, too, citing John Arden's remark: "Aston's story 'is highly detailed and circumstantial. But it is true? . . . '" (48),[1] and he continues to argue about Davies's sporadic hostility to Blacks that "Davies is certainly problematic as a vehicle for such a critique [of English racism]" (49).

Aside from Aston's story, if Davies's description of the monastery and his hostile references to Blacks are not to be trusted, a liberal humanist self itself as one of his identities also becomes fictive, not essential, as the self presupposes and depends on his remarks' truth. Back to the argument of the disguise motif, the first self, "the autonomous bourgeois monad or ego" (Jameson 15) which the first identity, Davies, seems to have represented would be considered to be fictive, not real.

2

What can we see in the second identity, Jenkins as tramp, which the disguise brings forth? What self is observable in the assumed Jenkins? He thinks his position or role as tramp is temporary. He says, "I might have been on the road a few years." As "I left them ['my papers'] with him ['A man I know']" at Sidcup, "I'm stuck without them" (29), but "If only I could get down to Sidcup," he can "sort all that out" (29). While he is a wandering tramp, he is, as it were, a runaway, too.

> DAVIES. I got an insurance card here. . . . Under the name of Jenkins . . . . It's got four stamps on it. . . . But I can't go along with these. That's not my real name, they'd find out, they'd have me in the nick. (29)

When he is offered the job of caretaker by Aston, and hears from him that "I could fit a bell at the bottom," so that "you could answer any queries" (52), he refuses to fit a bell, being afraid of his pursuers: "I'd go down there, open the door, who might be there. . . . They might be there after my card" (52-53). Thus we know that he lives in fear and anxiety every day; moreover he is also put in alienation. When he was working at the restaurant— "Ten minutes off for a tea-break in the middle of the night in that place and I couldn't find a seat, not one . . . all them aliens had it" (17)—only he was excluded from company. This situation in which he is put now is undoubtedly that of the "new" modernity to which Baumer refers (402).

It is needless to say that this world is that of modernism where the self is no longer seen as unified and essential, but split or incoherent and becomes fictitious.[2] It is this kind of self that we can observe in Jenkins, the second identity by disguise. As Baumer argues "this situation [the new modernity] gave European man [the opportunity] to improvise and create" (403), so Jenkins improvises stories as if he were a modernist. He is called a liar at last by Mick: "I can take nothing you say at face value. Every word you speak is open to any number of different interpretations. Most of what you say is lies" (82).

As Lois G. Gordon says the tramp "introduces himself as Davies to Aston, but as Jenkins to Mick" (42). He describes to Aston the inhuman experience in the monastery as Davies, but as Jenkins he might have created the stories like the monastery anecdote. Jenkins as improviser is very often glimpsed in his casual speeches. In order to testify to his cleanness he says he "left [his] wife" a fortnight after he married, because she put a "pile of her underclothing, unwashed" into the "pan for vegetables" (18), but the story is doubtful because he doesn't show an obsession with cleanliness later, replying nonchalantly, "Don't you worry about that" when Aston says "The blanket'll be a bit dusty" (27-28). He says to Aston, "I might get down to Wembley later on in the day" because in a cafe "they were a bit short-handed" and "want an Englishman to pour their tea" (36). However, to Aston's later question "How did you get on at Wembley," he replies, "Well, I didn't get down there" (48). Clearly he improvised the story about Wembly. He is a liar. Mick who suspects Jenkins is a liar leads him on in order to reveal his improvisations.

> MICK. You been in the services. You can tell by your stance.
> DAVIES. Oh . . . yes. Spent half my life there, man. Overseas. . . .
> MICK. In the colonies, weren't you?
> DAVIES. I was over there. I was one of the first over there. (59-60)

Mick functions through the drama as a medium by which the actual state of Jenkins or the self in him is illuminated. When Mick hears an old tramp's name is "Jenkins" (39) for the first time, he says, "You remind me of my uncle's brother" (40):

> He was always on the move, that man. . . . Had a funny habit of carrying his fiddle on his back. Like a papoose. I think there was a bit of the Red Indian in him. . . . I've never made out how he came to be my uncle's brother. I've often thought that maybe it was the other way round. I mean that my uncle was his brother and he was my uncle. . . . You spitting image he was. (40)

Jenkins is said to resemble Mick's uncle's brother whose identity is very enigmatic. But is the man really his uncle, or a blood relative? Is he British or a foreigner? Further, Mick says, "you've got a funny kind of resemblance to a bloke I once knew in Shoreditch" who "lived in Aldgate . . . was brought up in Putney . . . was born in the Caledonian Road" (41), and he continues his resemblance game, saying, "you remind me of a bloke I bumped into once, just the other side of the Guildford by-pass" (43). With the variety of Jenkins's doubles, a sense of unreality in them and their geographical diversity suggest Jenkins's incoherent or decentralized self. His self is literally fictitious as his disguise as Jenkins symbolizes.

But is Jenkins as tramp only a role, like a fiction with no reality? Here we have a hint of an answer to this question from the motif of boots which is found throughout the drama, namely, in Jenkins's persistent search for a pair of shoes just right for him, in which he wants to go to Sidcup. Begley compares the boots in Van Gogh's painting *A Pair of Boots* (1887) with "my old ones [broken-down shoes]" (24), which the tramp Jenkins tries to substitute for new ones at the monastery. According to Begley,

> Van Gogh's painting first may be read as a restoration of the objective world of peasant toil and agrarian misery from which the boots were concretely derived. This first stage we might call a realist gesture. (59)

Begley remarks the humanist iconography in this realistic reading of Van Gogh's boots and suggests that Pinter's mode of description of Davies's old shoes derives from Van Gogh's humanism.

> The familiarity of the humanist iconography surrounding old shoes is partly the result of painters like Van Gogh, and traditional values concerning poverty and degradation are forcefully recalled in Davies's retorts: 'What do you think I am, a dog? What do you think I am, a wild animal?' Like Van Gogh, Pinter seems to be marshalling the potent force of modernist synecdoche—using the shoes as markers of a long-lived experience of suffering . . . . (62)

As Begley puts it, it would be certain that Jenkins or Davies, who assumes the role of tramp, wandered "the expressways near Hendon and around London in search of forgotten friends, employment, and sustenance" (62), and daily goods such as soap and shoes.

> DAVIES. I was never without a piece of soap, whenever I happened to be knocking about the Shepherd's Bush area. (22)

> DAVIES. . . . it's taken me three days to get here, I said to him, three days without a bite . . . I . . . picked up a pair there. Got

onto the North circular, just past Hendon, the sole come off, right where I was walking. (23-24)

From such a realistic mode of reading as in the case of Van Gogh's boots, Jenkins's miserable life would be true and would confirm the reality of the humanist self in him. With respect to the monastery anecdote by Davies / Jenkins, Begley argues: "Davies certainly comes across as an inveterate liar. . . . At war with the wild implausibility of what is recounted, however, is the authentic indignation and puzzlement emanating from the speech" (61). If Begley's insistence on the authenticity in the tramp's anger at the monk's abuse is right, in spite of his recognition of the falsehood of Jenkins's speech, the fictitious identity or self born of disguise turns out to be a true one. A false self has changed into a true one.

3

This kind of paradox as to disguise has a precedent in a *fin-de-siècle* British drama. It can be seen in Wilde's *The Importance of Being Earnest* (1895), where Jack disguises himself as Ernest. In this disguise, the first identity is Jack Worthing, which must be true, to speak properly, but is false or fictitious. The reason is that when he was a baby, he was found in a hand-bag left in a cloak room at Victoria Station by Thomas Cardew, who "happened to have a first-class ticket for Worthing" (333), and named him Jack Worthing. Jack, who is "serious" and "has a higher sense of duty and responsibility" (340) in his country, disguises himself as "profligate Ernest" (336) when he comes up to London and associates with Algernon, a dandy. Ernest, the second identity, born of disguise, is a fictitious one, but it turns out to be a true identity in the denouement:

> JACK. Now, what name was I given?
>
> LADY BRACKNELL. Being the eldest son you were naturally christened after your father.
>
> . . . .
>
> LADY BRACKNELL. Yes, I remember now that the General was called Ernest. (382-83)

This disguise pattern shows paradoxically that the first identity, which must be true, is a false one whereas the second, the assumed one, is the true one. This paradox reminds us of Wilde's aesthetic "third doctrine." It is the doctrine that "Life imitates Art" ("Decay" 992). This doctrine can be paraphrased as reality ("Life") comes from fiction ("Art"). In Jack Worthing's case, a real identity comes from a fictitious one, Ernest. This disguise pattern makes its novelty conspicuous when compared with the preceding ones in British drama history. Here we'd like to look back at the tradition of disguise.[3]

The first pattern is observable in dramas in the age of the Renaissance when man is still considered to be a microcosm reflecting the macrocosm. In this era the self has the unified multiplicity which reflects the ultimate One like the Protean man in Pico's *Oration on the Dignity of Man,* as seen in the introduction. The disguise motif in this era reflects this type of man. Therefore, both the first identity or an inherent self and the second identity or an assumed self in disguise are true, not fictitious. "As the body revealed the soul, so appearance should reveal the truth of identity" (Bradbrook, "Shakespeare" 166) in this era. The two selves are united as *discordia concors.* In *The Merchant of Venice*, Portia who disguises herself as the lawyer Balthazar, becomes androgynous, her feminine identity and the assumed masculine one being combined. Portia/Balthazar as microcosm, reflects the macrocosm or the One. In this era the cosmic order was seen as embodying the Ideas according to teleological thinking.

On the other hand, when the mechanistic Newtonian world supplants the world of the chain of being, the view of man changes. Its change has a close relation to the emergence of liberal humanism. According to Catherine Belsey, "Liberal humanism, laying claim to be both natural and universal, was produced in the interests of the bourgeois class which came to power in the second half of the seventeenth century" (7). Though Jonathan Dollimore argues that this "essentialist humanism . . . only really emerges in the Enlightenment" (156), it produces the "liberal humanist self," as referred to above, and it is pervasive till almost the end of the nineteenth century. Baumer calls this period of a new world and a new man or self "'old' modernity," in contrast with "'new' modernity" which followed the twentieth century scientific revolution (402).

To return to the motif of disguise, this period engenders the second type of disguise. The first identity or the original self in disguise is essential or true whereas the second one or the assumed self is fictitious or false. Disguise, as it were, represents "Kant's duality of noumenal and phenomenal selves" (Eagleton 90).[4] In other words disguise hides the true or essential self, and shows the temporary or false one, but the noumenal self is seen through. This disguise sometimes takes the form of transparent disguise. It can be observed in Shakespeare's final romances.

> With the final romances . . . their disguises become transparent. In *Cymbeline* . . . Imogen in her page's disguise, her brothers and Belarious disguised as peasants, Cloten in Posthumus' garments, and Posthumus himself, as the poor soldier, change their habits merely; the characters are constant. So in *The Winter's Tale* the royalty of Perdita shows through her lowly habits. . . . (Bradbrook,

Growth 93)

Bradbrook's argument suggests that these characters' noumenal selves are constant or essential despite their disguise, whereas their assumed or phenomenal selves by disguise are only appearances or constructs.[5] William Wycherley also uses this transparent disguise. In *The Country Wife* (1675), Pinchwife makes her wife Margery disguise herself as her brother to prevent her infidelity, but the rakish Horner sees through her female identity under her male disguise, and kisses 'him,' saying, "give her [Margery] this kiss from me" (3.2.484).

In this way consideration of a tradition of disguise makes us guess that the disguise motif has a close relation to the view of the world and man contemporaneous with each type of disguise. It seems that Wilde's disguise also reflects such a background, and its novelty makes us perceive a symptom of the radical change of thought or the new modernity. The age of the new modernity is one of double awareness. By the twentieth century scientific revolution the external world which had been considered to be absolute and mechanistic proved to be illusory. Though a table was thought to be solid plane till then, the knowledge was false. A table turns out to be "a mass of moving particles" (Bell 12) according to the new science, and we have learned to accept "the recognition that science is a construction of the human mind before it is a reflection of the world" (Bell 11). This recognition suggests that the world is seen and caught subjectively, and the real comes from the subjective. To say simply, reality is born of fiction. Ernest in Wilde foretells this new view.

But Bell says that the "physicist continues to live in the Newtonian world of the layman" (12). This idea being applied to literature, it can be said that a writer lives in the world of realism. Wilde lives there too, and tries to realize Jack's "self-development" as in the nineteenth century *Bildungsroman*. But he does it through disguise. He develops Jack's self into Ernest's, and as Ernest is similar to Algernon in his dandyism, Ernest's self is a dandy's. Wilde says about a selfish man[6] "the primary aim of his life is self-development" ("Soul" 1101). Susan Laity argues that "*Earnest* concerns the self-realization of the individual, the development of the soul" (135), and adds that "Jack must develop *into* a dandy" (135). Ernest was the potential Algernon. Algernon's disguise as Ernest would prove this potentiality. For Algernon, who takes an interest in Cecily, disguises himself as Ernest, calling it "Bunburying" (338), and goes to see her in Woolton. Algernon, like Jack, disguises himself as the same 'Ernest.' Surely the correspondence of two persons through disguise or 'Ernest' confirms Jack's self-realization as a double of Algernon's self. In this way, the real Ernest or self is born of the false Ernest or self by way of disguise. This disguise in Wilde is clearly different from that in the era of the old modernity where the second self that disguise produces is literally false much like the new identity produced by Margery's disguise as her brother in *The Country Wife*.

4

We have argued so far that the Davies's disguise as Jenkins, a tramp in Pinter, is similar to Jack's disguise as Ernest in Wilde, in the sense that the first or original identity or self is false whereas the second one is true. In other words, among the two selves in disguise, the 'real' self is false while the fictitious self is true.

But is the type of disguise in Pinter the same as that in Wilde? Does Davies's self develop into Jenkins's by way of disguise? The answer is no. One of the reasons is that there is no idea of self-development in Pinter's drama, and another is that as there is a problem of "the difficulty, or indeed, impossibility of verification" in Pinter (Esslin, "Harold Pinter's Theatre" 34), we can't verify which identity is true identity, Davies or Jenkins. The third is a principle of modernist negation.

Though we might discern the humanist self in Davies /Jenkins from the realist reading, we also detect the incoherent or split self in him from modernist negation. This is because all of Jenkins's/Davies's utterances are doubtful in truth. As to our interpretation of his speeches, Begley argues, "the hermeneutic gesture begins to encounter resistance. A realism of old men walking Hendon expressways? Of discourteous monks? " (62). There is a comical example in which his lie and split self are combined. When Jenkins /Davies tries to win Mick's favour to banish Aston from Mick's house without letting him rebuild it, he pretends to be an interior decorator who rebuilds Mick's house in Aston's stead: "I could decorate it out for you, I could give you a hand in doing it . . ." (72). But afterwards when Mick says "you say you're an interior decorator," he denies his words: "I never touched that. I never been that" (80-81). Mick who sees through the "bloody poster" (81) in Davies /Jenkins inflates his identity as interior decorator more and more exaggeratedly.

> MICK.   . . . I want a first-class experienced interior decorator. I thought you were one.
>   . . . .
> MICK.   . . . I understood you were an experienced first-class professional interior and exterior decorator.
>   . . . .
> MICK.   You wouldn't be able to decorate out a table in afro-mosia teak veneer, an armchair in oatmeal tweed and a beech frame settee with a woven sea-grass seat? (81)

Jenkins/Davies, upon whom this swollen or unknown self has been thrust, cries at last: "I never said that!" (81). This is, as it were, an image of his alter ego who begins to walk beyond his control. This is a comical caricature of the division of his self as is seen in his pretension as an interior decorator. Or it is an absurdly comical proliferation of his self.[7] Generally speaking, he pretends to be a multiple man. When Aston suggests he was tempted by a girl in a café ("she said, how would you like me to have a look at your body? " [34]), he pretends to be a gigolo ("Women? There's many a time they've come up to me and asked me more or less the same question" [34]) while he feigns to be a specialist in shoes and clothes: "Suede goes off, it creases, it stains for life in five minutes. You can't beat leather" (24) or "I know about these sort of shirts . . . . Shirts like these, they don't go far in the winter time" (50). But his multiplicity isn't unified, but scattered. His self as tramp is split, and now to his bafflement another false self has been absurdly thrust upon him from outside. Mick points out how his self is split or inconsistent, saying ironically "You got two names. What about the rest?" (82).

This tramp's self is not only split diversely but also unsubstantial in nature. If so, are both Davies's self and Jenkins's self fictitious like the postmodern self? We'd like to say no to this question, too. We must read this drama in two modes of realism and modernist negation and in view of the exchangeability of the two selves in disguise, the first seemingly true identity and second assumed false one, deriving from Pinter's insistence on the impossibility of distinction between truth and falsehood. Seen from the realistic mode, each self shows an aspect of the humanist self whereas each presents the split or inconsistent self, seen from the mode of modernist negation. Disguise in *The Caretaker* can be maintained to be a state in which each self becomes both true or essential and fictitious or constructed. It isn't a type of postmodern disguise. In postmodern disguise, "personal identity is not conceived as essentially or originally present . . ." (Davis 4). This postmodern type of disguise would represent the disunited multiplicity or split of the self. It suggests that each self in the two selves born of disguise is fictitious. Disguise in *The Caretaker*, as it were, can be asserted to be located in between Wilde's type of disguise and the postmodern one. Each self in disguise can be both true and false in the play. We must remember one of Pinter's famous sayings: "A thing is not necessarily either true or false; it can be both true and false" ("Writing for the Theatre" 11).

Notes
1. This quotation from John Arden by Begley is taken from Billington 128.
2. Baumer says, "Not only Beckett but many of the best known figures of contemporary European literature wrote . . . of a vanishing self, an incoherent self, a decentralized self, of a self that possibly did not even exist" (420).
3. See Hosokawa 33-64.
4. Catherine Belsey sees the emergence of the liberal humanist subject (noumenal self) in Richard Brathwait's *The English Gentleman* (1630), and says that Brathwait argues that noumenal self is to the phenomenal one what the sun is to clouds, which hide the sun transitorily.

   > Brathwait . . . asserts . . . the diachronic continuity of the subject. People may seem to change, he insists, but this is simply a matter of appearances, like clouds covering the sun. In time people's true dispositions emerge and these are unalterable, 'being so inherent in the subject, as they may be moved, but not removed.' (34)

5. As to transparent disguise in *Cymbelline* (1609-10), *The Winter's Tale* (1610-11), *and The Tempest* (1611-12) in Shakespeare's romances, see Hosokawa 341-409.
6. Wilde describes a selfish man as follows: "a man is called selfish if he lives in the manner that seems to him most suitable for the full realization of his own personality" ("Soul" 1101).
7. A situation similar to this occurs in Algernon's disguise as Ernest in *The*

Importance of Being Earnest. Algernon as Ernest is visited by a solicitor, Gribsby, "at the suit of the Savoy Hotel Co. Limited for £762 14*s*. 2*d*." for dinners there (349), and he says, perplexed, "I never dine at the Savoy at my own expense" (350), but another Ernest as whom Jack disguises himself dines there. Algernon as Ernest, as it were, comically encounters the alter ego out of hand. We can see a similar case in Shakespeare's disguise of doubles or twins although the dramatic effects are a little different. The disguise of doubles is included in a type of disguise which is defined as the substitution of dramatic identity or the mistaken identity (Bradbrook, "Shakespeare" 159, 160). In *The Comedy of Errors*, Antipholus of Syracuse, a younger brother of twins, is mistaken for his elder brother, Antipholus of Ephesus, and forces his brother to incur comically a series of misfortunes, where his brother is shut out of his house and suffers wrongs such as exorcism by his wife, who mistakes the younger brother for her husband.

3
Double Awareness and the Self in *The Collection* and *The Lover*

Though a double awareness of a Newtonian "realism" and an X ray illusoriness or fictitiousness is applied to the modernist writer's recognition of the world by Michael Bell, it can also be applicable to Pinter's treatment of the self in *The Collection* (1961) and *The Lover* (1962). Concerning the relation of modernism to the self, Charles Taylor says, "Twentieth-century art has gone more inward, has tended to explore . . . subjectivity. . . . But at the same time, it has often involved a decentring of the subject: . . . an art displacing the centre of interest onto . . . dissolving the self" (456). According to Taylor, the self was a unitary one in the nineteenth century. Modernists, who were in opposition to the world "seen just as mechanism" in the nineteenth century (456), had a view of the world "as experienced, known and transmuted in sensibility and consciousness" (460) and inevitably acquired an awareness of living on a duality or plurality of levels. To them the "recognition that we live on many levels has to be won against the presumptions of the unified self, controlling or expressive" (480).[1] The multileveled consciousness of life and the world leads to the fragmentation or multiplicity of the self. However, if as Michael Bell says, "the commonsense table continues to exist but only within a human scale of reference" (12), so too does the unified self exist in realist representation.

In *The Collection* and *The Lover*, it seems that Pinter is unfolding multiple, illusory selves in each person's narrative of his or her experience of things or in a game of role-playing or disguise, whereas the realistic representation of the characters seems to give us an impression that each also possesses a unified self. This chapter explores the self in both plays from the viewpoint of this 'double awareness,' while referring to Shakespeare, who also aimed at the representation of the multiplicity of the self using disguise.

1

One of Pinter's early dramas, *The Collection*, develops its action centering on an occurrence whose truth or falsehood is uncertain. The alleged event is one in which Stella, James's wife, and Bill, who are both dress designers, had illicit intercourse in a hotel in Leeds where they were away on business. The first version of this is offered by James, an account which is said to be based on his wife's confession. According to Stella's story (via James), Bill and Stella met in the lounge of the hotel and went to their respective rooms after some conversation. Afterwards, Bill visited her room under the pretext of having left his "toothpaste" behind (132), and "slept with her" (131), seducing her against her will (132). But Bill refutes Stella's story as conveyed by James, saying, "The truth . . . is that it never happened. . ." (136): they "got out of the lift, and then suddenly she was in [his] arms" and "just kissed a bit, only a few minutes, by the lift" (136). What is fact, what is true about this occurrence in Leeds? It is not only Stella's story and Bill's that are inconsistent regarding this event.

There are three more versions of this story. One of them insists that it is James's "fantastic story." The story which James tells to Bill is not Stella's, but is fabricated by him.

> STELLA. . . . my husband has suddenly dreamed up such a fantastic story, for no reason at all.
> HARRY. That's what I said it was. I said it was a fantastic story.

(148)

Another version insists that it is Stella's "Pure fantasy" (154). Harry who has come back from Stella's flat says to James and Bill, "What she confessed was . . . that she'd made the whole thing up" (154). This means that the event in Leeds was her own fabrication. The last version is Bill's new confession coming at the end of the drama. Bill remarks, "we sat . . . in the lounge . . . just talked . . . about what we would do . . . if we did get to her room . . . two hours . . . we never touched . . . we just talked about it. . ." (156-57). When we remember Pinter's insistence about his plays that "there can be no hard distinction . . . between what is true and what is false" ("Writing for the Theatre" 11), we suspect that it is not the verification of truth or falsehood about the event that comes into question here. Martin Esslin says, "Pinter himself does not, perhaps cannot, give the answer" (*Theatre* 253), concerning these stories. If so, what should we think of these different stories?

What is most important about these versions seems to be that the multiple phases of each character emerge from these different stories; in other words, the multiplicity of the self of each person who experienced the event either directly or indirectly unfolds incoherently. When James protests to Bill that he treated his wife "like a whore" (131), Bill's bestial and sexist self is disclosed. Truly, his bestiality is testified later by Harry who says, "There's something faintly putrid about him. . . . Like a slug" (155) and Bill himself shows his sexist self by pointing out the female nature of sensuality: "Every woman is bound to have an outburst of . . . wild sensuality. . . . It's part of their nature" (151). But his narrated version of the event, inversely, betrays Stella's sensual self (136), which is inconsistent with the self of the "devoted wife" (133). By proving her nonresistance at the alleged rape (132-33), he establishes his innocent self, and discloses the secret selves of Stella and James hidden under the mask of a happy marriage ("You're a chap who's been married for two years, aren't you, happily?" [151]). It is suggested that she has been unfaithful to her husband by Bill's ironic phrase, "You've got a devoted wife, haven't you?" (133), whereas James is a believer in his wife as a devoted self ("Do you know her well?" [136]).

When James, after meeting Bill, reports, in a new version of the events, to Stella that Bill confirmed her story, adding to it Bill's implication of her seduction (143), James says, "I found him quite charming," and, "He was ... a man's man" (143) in passionate praise of him. He finds in himself a homosexual self during his protest to Bill over the event. At the same time, he discovers sexism in Bill's imputation of the event to a woman's seduction ("Typical masculine thing to say" [143]), but he is such a person himself, too. James feels a homosocial relation to Bill, one which excludes women, and so admires his frank attitude by saying, "He's got the right attitude . . . . As a man, I can only admire it" (143). That is the reason why *"she covers her face, crying"* (143) after that. Afterwards, when James visits Bill again and Bill welcomes him, by preparing olives, which James likes (145), his new self is recognized. James later thanks her for being a mediator: "After two years of marriage it looks as though, by accident, you've opened up a whole new world for me" (144). Furthermore, in the two men's intimate conversation, Bill's multiple identities are suggested— "a very cultivated bloke," "a considerable intelligence," "a man of taste" (144) and a man interested in opera— through Hawkins, a friend in his school days, whom Bill has reminded James of. When we hear James say, ". . . only after meeting him . . . I can see it both ways, three ways, all ways . . . every way" (143-44), we understand that it is not only multifaceted views of things or the world, but also those of the self that he is referring to.

But James and Bill are very different persons in the unfolding of each self. This is illuminated by the mirror episode where the argument is about whether James is tall or broad. Bill insists that mirrors are "deceptive," whereas James says, "I don't think mirrors are deceptive" (146). The idea that mirrors are not deceptive but real can be linked to the Newtonian or nineteenth century worldviews, and to realism. Given that the self in realism is a unified one, James's self looks to be unified. On the contrary, Bill represents an X ray awareness of the world. To him, the reflections in the mirror are illusory.

2

The third and fourth versions of the events in Leeds in which the story itself is attributed to James's or Stella's fabrications make clear further what the couple's married life really is like, as well as the relationship between Harry and Bill, disclosing their own hidden selves. When Harry visits Stella in her husband's absence, he complains to her about James's bothering Bill with "some fantastic story" (148). Harry's appeal brings to light that James's fabrication has come from his recent "overwork" (148), solitude and jealousy when Stella, a new woman in business, had "been away. . . showing dresses" (148), and met Bill (143). But his anxiety about Bill's trouble reveals at the same time that Harry has both a patriarchal self and homosexual one. Harry "found him in a slum . . . gave him a roof, gave him a job," and they have "been close friends" since then (147). When he reports to James Stella's fabrication, his patriarchism is made visible by his sexist words to James: "If I were you I'd go home and knock her over the head with a saucepan and tell her not to make up such stories again" (154). It is manifest also from everyday life in which he makes Bill fix the stair rod or serve him breakfast (123-24). Harry can be considered to be the most consistent unified self of the four characters.

But his misrecognition of a grapefruit as a pineapple (123) leads us to suspect his belief in a Newtonian world. This doubt is strengthened by his unrealistic description of the external appearance of a visitor to Bill, who might be James.

> BILL. What did he look like?
> HARRY. Oh . . . lemon hair, nigger brown teeth, wooden leg, bottlegreen eyes and a toupee. (140)

This bizarre and varied image of the stranger is suggestive of the idea that the realism of modernists is not an objective one, but an interior or illusory one; therefore, it reflects or symbolizes the multiplicity of the interiority of Harry, who saw the stranger so.

Furthermore, the emergence of another self is suggested in the stage directions during a visit to Stella: "HARRY *sits next to* STELLA *and proceeds to pet and nuzzle the kitten. Fade flat to half light,*" following his words, "Oh, what a beautiful kitten . . . come here, kitty, kitty" (149), where the kitten symbolizes Stella. His hidden bisexual self appears here, though Guru Charan Behera insists that "His fondling of Stella's kitten indirectly suggests his attempt to come out of the unreal image of a dominating big brother and reach out to the natural impulse within him" (65), his homosexual impulse being purged. At the same time, it is suggested that Stella's sensual self, unsatisfied in her married life with James, has fulfilled its needs. This is referred to by Harry's later report to James that "she'd made the whole thing up. . . . For some odd reason of her own" (154). The reason was wish fulfillment due to her secret "wild sensuality" (151). Bill also points out her desire unsatisfied by James, saying to her husband, ". . . it may be the kind of sensuality of which you yourself have never been the fortunate recipient" (151).

Meanwhile, this fourth version of the story strengthens the image of James as a unitary self. He is a believer in a conventional system of values. Since he wants to believe in Stella as a devoted wife, he is "glad to hear that nothing did happen" (155). He is such a believer in people's words that he is apt to be logical, so he asks Bill why he "confirmed the whole of her story" (154) so far, whereas Bill's answer and Harry's explanation of his personality tell us realistically that Bill has a perverse self as a slum boy. Bill answers, "It amused me to do so" (154). "Because he's got a slum mind," Harry explains. "He confirms stupid sordid little stories just to amuse himself, while everyone else has to run round in circles to get to the root of the matter and smooth the whole thing out" (155). Though Harry discloses Bill's wicked nature reproachfully, it is also his patriarchal and caring attempt to guard and take him back from James, and reconcile both of them, who were just in a duel with knives.

But contrary to Harry's kind efforts, Bill narrates the fifth version of the event as "truth" (156), where he tells of Bill and Stella's innocence, and suspends the probability of their guilt. What is her response to this story? Although James wants Stella to acknowledge Bill's story ("You just sat and talked about what you would do if you went to your room" [157]), the stage directions at the end say: "STELLA *looks at him, neither confirming nor denying. Her face is friendly, sympathetic*" (157).

As for this version by Bill, we can say both that this is also a lie from his "slum mind" "to amuse himself," and that this is a truth, but whatever the facts of the case, there is no doubt that James and Stella's alienated married life is reconciled, judging from Stella's favorable demeanor; and the intimate relationship between Harry and Bill continues owing to Harry's tactful protection of Bill. A realistic awareness of this event would conclude the drama like this. But at the same time an X ray awareness of the events would confirm the probability of multiple selves in each character and the possibility of various kinds of lives due to them. The unfolding of multiple selves in each character by way of various narration of an event is similar to the use of disguise in Shakespeare. In *The Comedy of Errors* (1592-93), disguise due to a mix-up of the twins Antipholus of Ephesus and Antipholus of Syracuse generates a romantic and honest husband and a dishonest and tyrannical one in the two confused Antipholuses.[2] But there is an essential difference between the multiplicity of the self in Shakespeare and that in Pinter. In Shakespeare multiplicity is unified in man as a microcosm in the ontological order of the chain of being, while in Pinter's there is no unity ultimately; one is not united; the self is dispersed in a world which is a construction of the human mind, even though Pinter's characters seem to impress us as unitary selves in "the Newtonian world of layman" which "exist . . . only within a human scale of reference" (Bell 12), and in a realist aesthetic order.

3

In Shakespeare's romantic comedies such as *The Merchant of Venice* and *As You like it* (1599-1600), each heroine, Portia and Rosalind, disguises herself as a man, uniting femininity and masculinity into an ideal androgyny in which the multiplicity of the self is unified.[3] Disguise in Shakespeare "enlarges the original role and discovers its latent possibilities" (Bradbrook, *Growth* 88). We can find this kind of disguise in *The Lover*, where the couple Richard and Sarah carry on a role-play in which Richard disguises himself as her lover Max, while Sarah plays the role of a mistress who changes her clothes, without changing her name. They have a love affair in the afternoon. Their disguise or role-playing isn't limited to this game, but even in the game, Max and Sarah play one role after another, seeming to unfold their latent or constructed selves. The multiplicity of their selves is further amplified by their estimation of each partner. This last way of disclosing of the multiplicity of the self is the same as that in *The Collection*, as we have seen. But the multiplicity which is unfolded in their selves in such ways seems to come to be unified in both of them at the end of the play. Here, too, we can recognize an X ray awareness of the fictitiousness of the self as well as a realistic awareness of the unified self.

Because it isn't clear what the game of the affair is, an amusement or a wish fulfillment, the purpose of the game is also uncertain at first sight. When Sarah asks, "Who looked first?" Richard says, "You," while she denies it ("I don't think that's true" [169]). Whatever the truth is, we can only assume that there is disharmony in their married life, which is considered to be related to what their selves really are. They seem to be trying to improve their marriage through the game. In the morning and the evening, Richard is a serious businessman, wearing "*a bowler hat*" (161) and "*a sober suit*" (162), while, in the afternoon, he disguises himself as Max, a lover, with "*a suede jacket, and no tie*" on (175). Though it is true that his new self as lover contributes to the generation of his varied self, it also confirms that he is a conventional unitary man. Richard calls Sarah in the role of mistress a whore, "a common or garden slut" (167) to her shock. He is, as it were, a Victorian gentleman who divides women into the archetypal antithesis, mother or wife and whore. When Sarah sees in Richard a man who cares "so much for grace and elegance in women" (168), she points out one phase of Richard's antithetical view of women, which a sober Richard in the morning and evening represents. Richard, not Max, who is supposed to be "sitting at a desk going through balance sheets" (165) but yet meets a whore in the afternoon, displays the other extreme of the view and like a sexist expects in women only "someone who could express and engender lust with all lust's cunning" (169). He calls a whore, "a functionary who either pleases or displeases" (168). This antithesis is further emphasized in Richard's great praise of his wife, "Great pride, to walk with you as my wife on my arm. To see you smile, laugh, walk, talk, bend, be still" (187), and in Max's disdain of Sarah from a homosocial sexist, "We're both men. You're just a bloody woman" (183).

Though Richard plays Max, who represents a sexual self, he treats this self as if he were another person. At first he doesn't want to recognize him as his own. This can be discerned in his disgust for Max ("How nauseating") when Sarah says, "His whole body emanates love" (172). Such an alienating attitude to his alter ego discloses a hypocritical aspect of the conventional respectable man who tries to hide his bestial lust. As for sexuality here, Richard sees lust where Sarah sees love, and yet his disguise of the "Manly" (172) role, as Max, prefigures the development of bestial lust into passionate love. This is why Richard calls Sarah "You lovely whore" (196) at the end of the play, where Richard, a Victorian man of the morning and evening, and Max, a lover in the afternoon, unite in the evening, as Richard changes a sober jacket for a lover's.

4

Like Richard, Sarah also changes clothes in the afternoon, and displays different selves as in Shakespeare's romantic heroes. She wears *"a crisp, demure dress"* (161), and *"low-heeled shoes"* (166) in the morning and evening, while putting on *"a very tight, low-cut black dress"* (174) and *"high-heeled shoes"* (166), which are suitable for a mistress in the afternoon.[4] Though appearance represents one self in each of the couple, the relation of her two roles or appearances to the attached selves is very different from Richard's. The typical example can be seen in her wearing the wrong shoes in the evening. She is discovered wearing high-heeled shoes for the role of a mistress in the evening (166), which means that she joins the role of wife and mistress; in other words, she merges two selves in her, unlike Richard who separates them rigidly. Yet this doesn't always imply that the original self is mixed by a new self contrary to it. The new self is complementary to it. She thinks both selves have grace, elegance, and wit (168) and sees in his second self an additional lust related to new love. It is because she feels love for Richard through the illicit affair with Max that she says, "How could I forget you?" or "it's you I love"[5] (166), when asked if she recalls, during the affair, Richard at work. Therefore, she is shocked to hear that it is a lustful whore that Richard meets, regarding her as one, and so comments, "Sounds utterly sterile" (168) and "I'm sorry your affair possesses so little dignity" (169). It is true that she herself feels a sense of her unified self throughout the game, saying, "I think things are beautifully balanced" (173).

But this revealed inconsistency between two persons' recognition of the same affair and person would remind us of the modernists' view of the world as not an objective thing, but a construction of the human mind, as well as their view of man, whose self isn't already unified, but dissolved. The self as whore which Richard sees in Sarah, who plays a mistress, is also a potential self in her, which is actualized in a series of further games, as it were, a play within a play, performed by Max and his mistress Sarah during the affair. In this, both of them play roles which produce multiple selves disjointedly. At first, as a mistress Sarah plays a chaste wife waiting for her husband in the park, and is threatened with rape by a rude man played by Max. The feigned role reflects the wife Sarah, while Max's engenders the bestial self of Richard. During the crisis, Richard/Max/the villain changes into a "sweet" park keeper (178) who rescues her. This new man reflects "sweet" Max (172) whose sweetness anticipates Richard's (191), another alter ego. Then suddenly Sarah/mistress Sarah/a woman in the park seduces the park keeper like a whore, saying to the flinching man, "Can't you speak to strange girls?" and demanding a "cigarette" (178). This frank lust betrays her lustful self. To this, Richard/Max/the villain/the park keeper says, "Come here, Dolores" (178), to a whore who is back again to "a married woman" (179) in the park, and tries to assault her. At this stage, the identities of the man and the woman are obscured.

For all these, because the man says, "It's teatime, Mary" (179) after this, this last scene seems to return to the usual game of Max and mistress Sarah in the afternoon, despite the uncertainty of the identity of Mary. This is affirmed by Sarah's orgasmic cry, "Max!" following intercourse under the table, as in the ordinary afternoon game, as suggested by the stage directions (179). What this series of incoherent changes of identities and names in the affair implies is that the characters are unfolding their multiple selves, and revealing their fictitiousness as their appearance in fictional games suggests literally. We can discern a modernist alternative awareness of the self here, too.

5

The play afterwards, develops, as it were, realistically, despite its further use of role playing or disguise. At the beginning of the play, the two selves, Richard and Max were alienated, but after the scene of the consummation of desire, they are united; in other words, Richard appears through Max, or Richard becomes Max, or vice versa. To Sarah's surprise, Max suddenly offers to end their affair because of his reasonable concern for her husband, his wife and children. Correspondingly, Richard, who has come home in the evening, orders her to stop the affair on account of his "ignominy" (190), which was Max's reason, too (182). The identification of the two is also seen in Max's confession to his mistress Sarah that it is a "fulltime mistress" (182), not "Some spare-time whore"

(181) that he has got, saying, "I've been deceiving her [his wife] for years" (181). This is very true of Richard in the play. So she replies, "Yes, yes, you have" (182). Richard pretends to be "very well acquainted with a whore" (167), in spite of his actual meeting of a mistress. Later in the evening when Richard is usually a respectable businessman, he begins to be occupied with playing the bongo drums, which is a sexual symbol of the affair of Max and Sarah ("What fun" [194]), and reenacts, in the role of sexual seducer, the same 'play within a play' in the park that the two afternoon lovers were engaged in. Thus at the end of the play, Richard and Max are unified, as Elizabeth Sakellaridou points out,

> By resuming the lover's role in the clothes of the businessman and at the wrong time of the day and also by embracing his demurely-dressed wife as a whore, he tacitly accepts her wholeness and the integration of his own self. (104)

Richard no longer needs Max because sensuality and common sense or reason are united in his unified self. According to Charles Taylor, this unitary self is a romantic one which is "an ideal of perfect integration, in which both reason and sensuality . . . are harmonized " (480).

Meanwhile Sarah, who became disoriented by Richard's identification of her as a whore, and the refusal of the affair by Max and Richard, wasn't the ideal woman that Richard had praised: "I found them [dignity and sensibility] in you" (169). She was lacking domesticity, as is clear from her failure in cooking supper (164, 188). But she promises to cook (192) when Richard gets angry at her "falling down on . . . wifely duties" (188). This relationship seems to suggest the patriarchal ethos of the Victorian age, but it helps to expand the possibility of Sarah's already established multiple selves. With domesticity absorbed into her, Sarah, for the first time, in the evening when the role of respectable wife is expected of her, plays the role of mistress in the afternoon, which is mingled with a lascivious self affirmed in the play within a play reenacted with Richard. The stage directions say: *"She emerges from under the table and kneels at her feet, looking up. Her hand goes up his leg"*(195). The following change into clothes intended for the afternoon, from their evening ones, symbolizes the unification of their multiple selves.

> SARAH. You usually wear something else, don't you? Take off your jacket. . . . I'll change for you. (195-96)

This last unification in each of them would be both trustworthy and illusory because Richard and Sarah are real figures, not performed roles, and yet the change of clothes into those of the fictional afternoon roles insinuates the fictitiousness of their unified selves. Perhaps they will continue their married life more fully than before now that Richard has grown "adaptable" (172) and "mature" (178) as Sarah expected, and she has born the whole gamut of femininity, but the dispersion of multiple selves in them is transparent from an X ray awareness. In *The Lover*, too, a modernist double awareness is recognizable.

Concerning the last scene of the play, John Russell Taylor makes a similar point but from a different angle: "Richard and Sarah appreciate . . . the impossibility indeed of living together on any other terms except the acceptance of an infinitude of reflections in lieu of the unknowable, perhaps non-existent, essence" (350). As for Pinter's plays, he seems to paraphrase the modernist double awareness as follows: "In a world where everybody is the sum of so many reflections, where nobody is the same even to himself . . . for two seconds together, . . . we depend on the joint pretence that people have some sort of underlying consistency, and that perceptions can at least to some extent be relied on, in order to continue living at all" (352). To put this another way from the viewpoint of life, George E. Wellwarth says, in the case of *The Lover*, "Richard and Sarah live their real life, but they play variations on it and give these variations equal stature with their real, outward life while they are living them" (103). Though they have lived "as many lives as possible" (103), the couple's basic ordinary life has been enriched.

Notes
1. Charles Taylor explains the controlling unified self and the expressive self as follows:

   > The ideals of disengaged reason and of Romantic fulfillment both rely in different ways on a notion of the unitary self. The first requires a tight centre of control which dominates experience and is capable of constructing the orders of reason by which we can direct thought and life. The second sees the originally divided self come to unity in the alignment of sensibility and reason. (462)

   From another viewpoint, Eugene Lunn points out the integrated individual subject or personality in the nineteenth century as follows:

   > In both romantic and realist literature of the nineteenth century, individual characters are presented with highly structured personality features . . . . The narrator or playwright . . . endeavors to reveal integrated human characters . . . . (37)

   Incidentally, concerning the living of life on many levels, George E. Wellwarth says as follows:

   > The Absurdist measures life quantitatively as well as qualitatively *because life is all that there is*. To live as many lives as possible, no matter how temporarily, how spuriously, how self-deludingly, is to enrich the basic life we live. (103)

2. When Adriana, a wife of Antipholus of Ephesus discovers her husband's twin Antipholus of Syracuse, she says, "I see two husbands, or mine eyes deceive me" (5.1.331). In the disguise of the double, her husband's twin, whom she has mistaken for her husband, is both honest in wooing Luciana, and dishonest in betraying her. Antipholus of Syracuse is the latent Antipholus of Ephesus. "Adriana has indeed had two husbands—one who betrayed her and went mad in the process, and another who remained true" (Berry 75).
3. Cf. p. 43.
4. Noticing the change of their appearances such as clothes and shoes, Austin E. Quigley classifies the two aspects of Richard and Sarah's relationship as follows: "the public domain of a responsible husband-and-wife unit, and the private domain of two individuals with a passionate sexual bond" (83).
5. In this "you," Richard and Max are superimposed. This effect is the same as that born of double disguise by Rosalind in *As You Like It*. Whereas Rosalind is originally a chaste woman, she who disguises herself as Ganymede, plays 'Rosalind' in a game of wooing, who is secular and sexual. This is for the purpose of maturing Orlando secularly because his love for her is ideal and sacred. In that game, when she shows the sexual 'Rosalind' to him, and he refuses this image of her, saying, "my Rosalind is virtuous," she replies, "I am your Rosalind" (4. 1. 60, 62). In "your Rosalind," two Rosalinds, one secular and the other sacred, are superimposed.

4
Unity and Division of the Self in *The Homecoming*: Against Two Kinds of Realism

According to Michael Bell, the nineteenth century Newtonian realism (hereafter the first realism) is "the commonsensical or rational means of understanding them [external appearances]" which is "limited and fallible" (10), whereas the X ray view of the world (hereafter the second "realism") can see that the table, which the first realism believes is solid, is "'really' a mass of moving particles through which . . . it would be possible to penetrate without disturbance" (12).

When we examine the characters or the selves in Pinter's *The Homecoming* (1964), we recognize Pinter's sense of double awareness, of two kinds of realism. This awareness of the characters is like the anamorphic perspective which Holbein used in his picture, *The Ambassadors* (1533) in which something skewed in the bottom centre is transformed into a complete human skull, approached from another angle. The characters in *The Homecoming* also show different facets of the self when approached from both the front, the first realism, and from another angle, the second "realism." L.A.C. Dobrez develops a similar argument about two perspectives in Pinter's play. He introduces three epistemological perspectives for the whole work of Pinter up to *Betrayal* (1978). They are, firstly, the phenomenological or existential view, secondly, psychological realism, which is "obvious in the nineteenth-century novel . . . but is also observable in the drama of the naturalism of *Miss Julie* and the realism of Ibsen's middle period . . ." (335-36), and lastly, the extreme empiricist view, in which the "world becomes an incomprehensible

Newtonian body" (353), "the very notion of human identity is lost," and "People are just material presences and that is all" (352). The psychological realism Dobrez refers to seems to be the same as the first realism, and the third view corresponds to Bell's X ray perspective which we can call the second "realism." Though Dobrez calls this the Newtonian, it is certain that it is equivalent to Bell's X ray "realism" because this *"total empiricism"* (354) regards the world as "a world of atomic particles" (353) in the same way as the X ray epistemology sees a desk as a mass of moving particles. Dobrez perceives these two views in *The Homecoming*, but he insists that the extreme empiricist point of view is "Pinter's approach in *The Homecoming*" (352), remarking "Pinter's emphasis on the external" (352) in the play. Dobrez's recognition of this purely scientific view of the world would be right in terms of twentieth century epistemology, but he fails to see that its X ray "realism" reveals the illusoriness or fictiveness of the world, and therefore, in the modern arts, promotes the invention of the fictional—fantasies, dreams, memories and disguises— in order to remind people of the fictitiousness and emptiness of the world. *The Homecoming* has these kinds of illusory elements which indirectly derive from the X ray view, the second "realism," but these fictitious aspects, when some parts are strung together, seemingly look unified or true from the viewpoint of traditional realism or first realism which makes much of the cause and effect principle. Here is a difficulty in our appreciating *The Homecoming* and the characters or their selves. If we look at this drama and the characters only from the viewpoint of traditional realism based on a limited science within a human scale of reference, we might call the drama a "civilized jungle" as Bernand F. Dukore does ("Woman's Place" 237). But if we look at them from the viewpoint of two kinds of realism, we will confront a variety of selves or their divisions. Now we will examine, against the backgrounds of these viewpoints, the selves of three sons, Teddy, Lenny and Joey, and the enigmatic heroine Ruth.

1

When we compare *The Homecoming* with earlier plays such as *The Dumb Waiter* (1957), *A Slight Ache* (1958), *The Collection*, and *The Lover*, we soon perceive that it has only the realistic features of everyday life without any of the uncanny objects or actions like the grotesque dumb waiter which demands one dish after another, the mysterious figure of a silent matchseller, clear discrepancies between characters' utterances and the truth, or the queer disguised sexual games of a married couple. The plot is very simple. The eldest son, a Professor of Philosophy, Teddy comes back to his London house from America with his wife Ruth whom he married six years ago in secret. His family is a typical patriarchal one which his father, Max, rules and manages violently and scurrilously, including housework after the death of his wife, Jessie. We see frequent struggles for power between Max and his sons, Lenny and Joey, and between Max and his brother Sam. After the family's friendly reunion and all Max's momentary anger at the couple's secretive homecoming, Teddy finds he cannot adapt himself to his London family, so he soon determines to go back to America. But his family keeps Ruth back with the intention of making her their mother, their lover and a prostitute, to which Ruth agrees, though she attaches some conditions to it.

It goes without saying that Ruth's agreement to be a whore is abnormal when judged by commonsense. But it is possible that there might be such a person in this world, and we cannot categorically say that Ruth's existence is unrealistic. In short, though this family's way of living is aberrant, the representation of their life is within the realm of the nineteenth century realism. In fact the family comes from the nineteenth century patriarchal tradition. It is in the description of the dead mother, Jessie, that this is most conspicuous in the play. Max's description of her is very typical. On the one hand, he praises her in remembrance, saying "Every single bit of the moral code they [the sons] live by—was taught to them by their mother. . . . That woman was the backbone to this family" (62). She was, as it were, the angel of the family. On the other hand, she is despised and described as a whore, too. Max says, ". . . it made me sick just to look at her rotten stinking face" (25), and calls her "slutbitch" (63). Clearly such an antithetical view of a woman comes from the misogyny inherent to a patriarchy which derives from the medieval period, as Kent Cartwright points out: "Medieval morality plays such as *Mankind* (*c.* 1470) or Medwall's *Nature* (*c.* 1495) present women as temptations to sin or as embodiments of virtue. . . . The popular morality and saints plays . . . typically divide women into the opposing categories of whore and virgin" (135).

2

This realistic touch is clearly discernible in the representation of the personalities of the three sons and, needless to say, Max. Though Max is very violent and coarse, he is sensitive and sympathetic, too. At the start of the play, when Sam comes back from his work and continues to talk only with Lenny, Max edges himself into their conversation, saying "I'm here, too, you know"(28), feeling lonely. Max gets very angry in the morning when he finds out that Teddy has brought his wife secretly at night, but he demands a "cuddle" and kiss from him, when he hears that they have three sons (59). This behavior show that he has not only a full ego, a unified self, but also he has been depicted from the viewpoint of realism in the sense that his speech and conduct come from a causal relation, which is one of the features of the first realism. Max's exchange with Teddy is not an incomprehensible whim, but a reasonable one. As a patriarch, he is glad to know that the next patriarch has a successor.

This is true of the three sons, too. In the case of the youngest Joey, he is a boxer, but as Max says, "You don't know how to defend yourself, and . . . how to attack" (33): he isn't so strong. The cause is very simple. Joey is too tender and sympathetic as is clear from his sympathy for Teddy when Max gets angry at Teddy's secret homecoming ("You're an old man, [*To* TEDDY.] He's an old man" [58]). His tenderness is clear in his protection of Ruth who is called a "tease" (82), ("I didn't say she was a tease"). Among the three, the character of Lenny is very realistic. The conversation between him and Max at the beginning of the play draws attention to his full ego. He is defiant against Max's power, but he has no intention of overthrowing Max. He hopes to keep the family patriarchal. When he is asked by Max, "What have you done with the scissors?"(23), he first ignores it, and then says scornfully, "Why don't you shut up, you daft prat?" (23). Max gets angry at this, and makes a long speech about how he has a power superior to Lenny's (25-27), then he cunningly changes the topic of conversation twice, first to horse racing to calm his anger, second to Max's cooking: "LENNY. Honest. You think you're cooking for a lot of dogs" (27). But when Max strikes him with his stick, angry at his sarcasm, he apologizes like a child: "Dad, honest. Don't clout me with that stick, Dad" (27).

The episode of Teddy's theft of Lenny's cheese roll is typical of the play's causal realism. This episode occurs in Act II where, at the beginning, the old patriarch, Max, and the new one, Teddy, are reconciled, and the new harmony of the family is represented by their chatting over coffee made by Ruth, a substitute mother for Jessie. Max is very satisfied with this reunion, saying, "Well, it's a long time since the whole family was together, eh? . . . What would Jessie say if she was alive? Sitting here with her three sons. . . . And a lovely daughter-in-law" (61). In the midst of this happiness, Lenny asks Teddy a question of philosophy on "a certain logical incoherence in the central affirmations of Christian theism" (67) to show his respect for his brother, a Professor of Philosophy ("Your family looks up to you" [80], "a great source of pride to us" [81]). But unexpectedly Teddy cannot answer the question, and escapes from it, saying, "That question doesn't fall within my province" (67). Elin Diamond says, "by mocking philosophical ideas, the family makes his authority seem fraudulent" (153). It is in his revenge for this humiliation that he steals Lenny's cheese roll. Hearing his confession ("I ate it" [80]), Lenny says, "What led you to be so . . . vindictive against your own brother? " and recognizes that he has "grown a bit sulky during last six years" (80). Teddy's sudden proposal of going back to America after this episode (70) unfolds itself as the effect of a series of failed expectations and a sense of humiliation.

But whereas this causally realistic episode shows what a trivial action this is, we cannot believe its realism is reflected in the whole work. Diamond says that *The Homecoming* reflects life in a cracked mirror; in one fragment we recognize the familiar actions of family drama, in another fragment the same image is grotesquely distorted. . ." (140). She, too, confirms two perspectives in the play. Her "one fragment" corresponds to our first realism, while "another fragment" can be replaced by the X ray "realism." Though the selves of Joey, Lenny and Teddy seem to be consistent and unified from the commonsense viewpoint in this way, they turn out to be broken and become part of the ideal or complete self or man in general, looked at from the X ray view.

3

There are some scholars who regard each of three sons not as a unified self or a full ego, but as aspects or parts of a single personality or the self. Martin Esslin says,

> Lenny and Joey are complementary: Lenny slick and fast, Joey slow and strong, and they act as one. . . . In fact, these two could be seen as different aspects of one personality: Lenny embodying the younger son's cunning and cleverness, Joey his strength and sexual potency. (*Pinter* 142)

Incidentally, Esslin is also one of the critics who looks at this play from two angles, and in his case he sees "the perfect fusion of extreme realism with the quality of an archetypal dream image of wish fulfilment" (138) in the play. Vera M. Jiji explores this play in terms of "the ancient archaic rite" (101), and says "Like much modern art, poetry and drama, it may condense several figures into one, or it may split one figure into two or three who share some functional attributes" (102). Arthur Ganz develops almost the same argument as ours regarding the division of the self into three sons.

> . . . aspects of the self are broken up into separate entities—and particularly in the younger men, the Teddy-Lenny-Joey group. Bound together by their relationship as brothers (symbolic of their actual relationship as aspects of a single self) . . . they . . . encompass an unusual range of mind and temperament. (181)

But Ganz's view of "the triple self" has a contradiction. He points out Joey's partial "acting physical self" and Teddy's partial "intellectual self," whereas he regards Lenny's self as a "full ego" (182-83). In terms of the two kinds of realism, he seems to mix two perspectives. He sees only

Lenny in the light of traditional realism. From the X ray view, we suspect that his self also would be divided, and his self would be only part of the ideal self.

It is the inconsistencies among each of the three sons, and their sharing with each other which convince us that they stand for divisions of the self. Teddy is intelligent, but easily agrees to his family's absurd idea of his wife's becoming a prostitute (91), and, like a sexual technician, points out Joey's sexual immaturity when he hears "he didn't go the whole hog" in his flirtation with Ruth ("he hasn't got the right touch" [82]). In this point of sexual interest, his image overlaps with Lenny and Joey, who toy with Ruth. As for Lenny, he is cunning, active, and violent whereas he is interested in intellectual activity as is clear in his philosophical argument with Teddy (67-68), and is sexual, too, like Joey, in addition to his work as a pimp. His activeness and physical power are explained by his quick approach to Ruth (43-45) and two violent episodes concerned with women. In one episode, when he was at the docks, a woman approached him, and "made me a certain proposal," but as "she was falling apart with the pox" (46), he "clumped her one," and "gave her another belt in the nose . . . " (47). Another episode also shows these features of his when he "decided to do a bit of snow-clearing for the Borough Council" (48), and after the work, he was asked to move the iron mangle by an old woman, but he got angry at the woman for giving orders, so "gave her a short-arm jab to the belly" (49). Thus he overlaps with Teddy and Joey in the point of intelligence and power. As for Joey's overlapping traits with his brothers, we have mentioned the common features of sexuality and power above. These combinations of brothers in some features tell us that they are "each other," but they are a little different from each other. Dobrez recognizes such a relation among Davies, Aston and Mick in *The Caretaker* from a phenomenological point of view.

> Like the characters of *The Dwarfs* and *The Birthday Party*, Davies, Aston and Mick do not emerge as three separate Egos. . . . they are each other, in short, beings-there, beings-with. . . . they are not characters—in the usual sense—enacting a plot, but three men existing, living out the implications of their situation. (342)

On the other hand, he sees *The Homecoming* from the extreme empiricist viewpoint, and says, "Every character . . . is reduced to a material presence, every utterance to a vibration of particles . . ." (352). We approve, from the viewpoint of X ray "realism," the idea that each of three sons is not a separate Ego, but cannot agree with him that they are only a material presence. Their selves are broken, but are representative of a part of the ideal self which seems to derive from the Renaissance. Edgar Wind looks at Raphael's *Dream of Scipio* from an iconological point of view. Considering the book, sword and flower presented to Scipio by two women in the painting, Wind says:

> These three attributes . . . signify the three powers in the soul of man: intelligence, strength and sensibility, or. . . mind, courage, and desire. In the Platonic scheme of the 'tripartite life'. . . . Together they constitute a complete man. . . . 'The philosophers . . . have decided that the life of humanity consists of three parts, of which the first is called theoretical, the second practical, the third pleasurable: which in Latin are named *contemplativa, activa*, and *voluptaria*.' (81-82)

From Wind's argument, we can infer that the Western ideal of the unified self consists of intelligence (mind), strength (courage) and sensibility (desire), and that with the modern division of the self, its three parts are also dispersed. In this play, too, the notion of an ideal self cracks. It is what Lenny was expecting from Teddy, "a standard for us" (80): "a bit of grace . . . a bit of generosity of mind, a bit of liberality of spirit" (81). Can we, therefore, not argue that Teddy represents a theoretical fragment, Lenny a practical one, Joey a pleasurable one, each part of a unified self?

There is nothing to prove that Pinter was well versed in such Renaissance knowledge, but he was an actor who had performed in many plays by Shakespeare, whose work seems to be infused with such ideas. As is argued later, the influence of Shakespeare can be discerned behind this play. As for the characters' inconsistencies which cannot be understood by the first type of realism, archetypal criticism and Lacanian psychology have been applied so far,[1] but we regard their inconsistencies as reflections of the division of the unified, ideal self.

4

Dobrez who analyzes *The Homecoming* from the viewpoint of an extreme empiricist says, "Ruth is neither a being-in-the-world nor an Ego, only a mysterious *res* [thing]" (352). It is true that she is mysterious, but when we look at her in the light of two kinds of realism, she seems to be a new unified woman beyond the traditional patriarchal female image, while that unity is divided, with each fragment proving to be fictitious. As Jiji puts it, this play "may condense several figures into one" (102), and the only example is Ruth. Many critics regard her as mother, wife and prostitute. Victor L. Cahn says, "she will play the roles of wife, mother, whore, and mistress that fulfill all the desires these men have," though he recognizes "she is the ultimate figure of authority in this home" (72). When we hear Esslin say, "As the elder brother's–a father substitute's–wife, Ruth is a mother figure, she is a reincarnation of Jessie" (*Pinter* 143), and that "both

Jessie and Ruth are both mother and whore" (*Pinter* 144), we have confirmed that such an image of woman comes from patriarchal misogyny. Looked at from traditional realism, Ruth's story is as follows: a common model before marriage goes to America as a Professor's wife, and takes care of three sons as mother, serving her husband to "help [him] with [his] lectures " (71), only to find "all rock," "sand" and "lots of insects there" (69), so that she feels unsatisfied sexually, whereas, the rude London family welcome her passionately as a substitute for their dead mother, and the two sons try to meet her frustrated passion in place of her husband. The family aims to treat her as a new mother, wife ("She can have more [children])! Here" [86]), a mistress and a whore who "can earn the money herself" (88). She chooses to remain as a new "backbone to this family" (62), rather than "a great help" (66) to her husband, since some proposed terms of the contract have been accepted such as the number of rooms. This realistic reading would reinforce the power of traditional patriarchy.

But some critics see that this combination of women's roles helps to make her complete or whole. Elizabeth Sakellaridou notices her development in the play, saying, "By the end of the play she has formed for herself a compact personality, synthesising all the aspects of the female principle, the mother, the wife and the whore. . . . in the final stage she reaches her self-completion" (111). Ganz asserts that "each woman—though embodied in a single presence—plays three different roles: She is at once wife, mother, and a prostitute" (181), and declares, "Pinter suggests that the reverence and affection granted the mother can never be dissociated from the lust aroused by the mistress" (185).

This union of opposites, virtue and lust, in a woman reminds us of Raphael's *The Three Graces* in which Beauty is in the centre with Castitas (chastity) on the left and Voluptas (lust) on the right. "Beauty holds the balance between them, being chaste and pleasurable in one " (Wind 80). In the Renaissance, beauty was considered to be the union of chastity and lust (pleasure), reflecting the Platonic definition of beauty as "Love combined with Chastity" (Wind 73), and the ideal woman is the combination of Pallas (wisdom), Juno (power) and Venus (pleasure). Pinter may not have known of the Renaissance ideal woman, but such a woman often appears in Shakespeare, especially as a heroine disguised as man, like Portia in *The Merchant of Venice* and Rosalind in *As You Like It*. They combine an innate chastity with intellect and the power acquired by their masculine disguise, and give pleasure, too, like Beauty in Raphael's picture. Portia's chastity as a wife is clear from her words, "her gentle spirit / Commits itself to yours to be directed, / As from her lord . . ." (3. 2. 163-65), while her lustful aspect is discernible in her words "I will become as liberal as you, / I'll not deny him any thing I have, / No, not my body, nor my husband's bed: / Know him I shall" (5.1. 226-29). As for Rosalind, the Duke's words "her smoothness, / Her very silence, and her patience / Speak to the people" (1.3. 73-75) testify to her female virtue; her idea and practice of the love game in which she matures Orlando in love indicate her intellect and power, while as Ganymede she plays the role of 'sexual Rosalind,' and betrays the reality of her hidden sexuality ("I will be . . . more new-fangled than an ape, more giddy in my desires than a monkey" 4. 1. 141-45). Significantly, Pinter himself appeared as an actor in both *The Merchant of Venice*, and *As YouLike It*. He played Bassanio in 1951-2 and late 1953 with Anew McMaster in Ireland, and Salanio in 1953 with Donald Wolfit at the King's Theatre, Hammersmith, and as for the latter, in the same period, he acted as Charles the Wrestler and Jaques de Boys.[2] There is little doubt that he knew from this experience before he wrote this play (1964) that a woman with such a combination of opposing traits could be an ideal woman, a unified but multiple self.

5

We are back to Ruth now in order to investigate what the three aspects of a woman, three aspects of an ideal self, are like in her. Ruth in Act I gives us a glimpse of motherhood, intellect and lust. Her consciousness of motherhood appears twice, first toward the sons in America, and second toward Lenny. When Teddy and she arrive at the London family, Ruth worries first about their children ("the children . . . might be missing us" [38]), while Teddy is inattentive due to the joy of his homecoming. After Teddy goes to bed, Lenny is eager to approach her, telling stories of his past and offering a drink of water, but she shows intellect in the way she pierces the fabrication of his stories and his frustrated hunger for a mother and a woman. Her sharp question, "How did you know she was diseased?" (47) reveals the fiction of the story of a whore "with the pox" (46), drawing out his confession, "I decided she was" (47). Further, detecting his childish frustration with women in his violence against the two women in the fabricated stories, she calls him "Leonard," which is "the name my mother gave me" (49), and says "If you take the glass . . . I'll take you," when he tries to remove her glass of water (50). She tries to lure him sexually, but her tempting is a mixture of sexuality and maternal affection, because her action makes us think of a mother taking care of a baby who lies on its back ("Lie on the floor. . . . I'll pour it [water] down your throat" 50). With Lenny perplexed at her behaviour, she says, "Oh, I was thirsty" (51), after *She laughs shortly, drains the glass* " (50). Her simple comment tells us that she did not mean to lure him, but only wanted to drink the water, pretending to take care of a baby, though it is certain that her word "thirsty" connotes her thirst for unsatisfied lust in America, too. Affection and chastity in a mother and lust in a wife are mixed here.

In Act II, Ruth continues to display these phases of an ideal woman or self, which proves to be the ideal for which patriarchy longs in women. This is demonstrated by the patriarch, Max, who is pleased with Ruth's cooking ("I'm not bad" 61), and who praises the dead wife, Jessie as "a woman . . . with a will of iron, a heart of gold and a mind " (62). Needless to say, Jessie couldn't attain the ideal, for she was an unfaithful woman who had a secret affair with Max's bosom friend, as Sam confesses at the end of the play ("MacGregor had Jessie in the back of my cab" [94]). And now, Ruth embodies the ideal figure of a woman, succeeding Jessie as a mother to the patriarchal family. "A will of iron" is equivalent to power, "a heart of gold" to love (lust), and "a mind" to intellect. If the misogynistic view of a woman, seen in Max's earlier description of Jessie, is realistic in patriarchy, the Renaissance view can be an ideal aspiration for a woman. As if fulfilling their aspiration, Ruth shows herself a dutiful wife in speaking of her husband's worries on behalf of Teddy ("I think he wondered whether you would be pleased with me" [65]), and demonstrates a flash of wit in Lenny's question, "Philosophically speaking. What is it [table]?"(68). She answers,

> You've forgotten something. Look at me. I . . . move my leg. That's all it is. But I wear . . . underwear . . . which moves with me . . . it . . . captures your attention. Perhaps you misinterpret. The action is simple. It's a leg . . . moving. (68-69)

According to Dobrez, Ruth is "supporting her husband" (351) who answers, "A table" (68), and answers as if she said, "Things, whether tables or moving legs, are just things. Why foist human interpretations, subjective emotions on them? Why not just accept the simple, natural material presence of things?" (Dobrez 351). Judging from Dobrez's identifying of Ruth as an extreme empiricist who see things without human connotations (352-53), from the viewpoint of X ray "realism," we can understand her objective insight into Max's vain obsession with the happy patriarchal family. Max, after lunch, exultantly relates his remembrance of "negotiations with a top-class group of butchers with continental connections" (62) and how great the whole family's happiness was made on that day (62). Ruth, hearing that, says, "What happened to the group of butchers?" (63) to which Max answers, "They turned out to be a bunch of criminals like everyone else" (63) thereby confessing the vain subjective fantasy of this happy family story, which she has already seen through.

The relationship between Ruth and Joey can be explained by her simple intelligence and maternal affection. Joey's lack of intelligence, which draws attention to Ruth's, is quite obvious in his errors of grammar ("No, he don't" [85]). His childishness and hunger for maternal affection is shown in his first line in the play, "Feel a bit hungry," and Max's response to it: "Go and find yourself a mother" (32). The combination of these elements in the relationship between the two characters is represented in a series of actions in the play, not in the realistic description of details. Hearing the first familiar conversation between them, Max says, "He speaks so easily to his sister-in-law, do you notice? That's because she's an intelligent and sympathetic woman" (67), and his next words to Teddy are symbolic of their relationship: "Eh, tell me, do you think the children are missing their mother?" (67). This is the moment when Ruth becomes a mother to Joey, who is missing his real mother. An embrace in front of the family after that (75-76) and sexual affairs upstairs are a mixture of a mother-son affection and love (lust). As for the latter, love, Joey who succeeds Lenny in caressing her embodies Lenny's love. Before Joey robs Lenny of Ruth's kisses, Ruth lays bare her soul to Lenny for the first time in the play (72-74), and their love is suggested when Lenny proposes a dance with her.

Uniting intellect and passion, Ruth starts to use her power while being absorbed into the patriarchal London family: after "RUTH *suddenly pushes* JOEY *away*" in their caress on the floor (76), Ruth orders Joey and Lenny to bring food, a drink and a proper glass:

> LENNY. What drink?
> RUTH. Whisky.
> ....
> RUTH. What's this glass? I can't drink out of this. Haven't you got a tumbler?
> ....
> JOEY. What food do you want?   (76-77)

From the viewpoint of traditional realism, this kind of power is plausible in the sense that it is similar to Jessie's command over the household as "the backbone to this family," which the patriarch Max praises. But when we confront Ruth's demands in the contract for a prostitute, we sense her power differently.

6

Though the family never utters the word 'prostitute' to Ruth, she realizes their intention, asking, "A flat?" when Lenny says to her "We'd get you a flat" (92). After this, she demands one term after another such as "three rooms and a bathroom," "a dressing-room, a rest-room, and a bedroom" (92), "A personal maid?"(93), and as soon as Lenny begins to use the terminology of economics such as "finance you," "pay us back, in instalments" (93). she also begins to use masculine terms of contract, law and economics, and takes the lead in the contract:

RUTH. You would have to regard your original outlay simply as a capital investment.

. . . .

RUTH. I would naturally want to draw up an inventory of everything I would need, which would require your signatures in the presence of witnesses.

LENNY. Naturally.

RUTH. All aspects of the agreement and conditions of employment would have to be clarified to our mutual satisfaction before we finalized the contract.

LENNY. Of course. (93)

Marc Silverstein, adopting Luce Irigaray's term, "*mimicry*" (Irigaray 76), says, "Pinter here describes a kind of mimetic practice, a deliberate assumption of the role to which patriarchy consigns women that transforms subjection into empowerment" (77-78). We agree with his comment about her obeying the patriarchal family's plan, while ruling them, adopting the patriarchal principle, but we further advance the argument, from her making use of Lenny's usage, a masculine one, and insist that she is disguising herself as a prostitute, as Portia disguises herself as a lawyer, using the terms of law in the judgment scene.

From the viewpoint of disguise, Ruth is not Portia, but rather Katherina in *The Taming of the Shrew* (1593-94), and indeed it can be said that the final scene of *The Homecoming* is influenced by that of *The Taming of the Shrew*. The cogent evidence is the final words of Max, "kiss me" (98). They remind us of Petruchio's "kiss me, Kate" (5. 2. 181). Petruchio utters these words triumphantly after Katherina makes a speech to the effect that a wife or a woman should obey a husband or a man (5.

2.137-80). The patriarch Petruchio is glad to know that Katherina, who was a defiant shrew, has been tamed into a woman loyal to the patriarchy. However, the style and content of her speech suggest her resistance and disobedience to him, she pretending to be an obedient woman.[3] Her long speech proves that "she assumes the role of a preacher whose authority and wisdom are . . . thoroughly masculine" (Kahn 116), violating the traditional virtue of silence or short speech demanded of a faithful woman (Cartwright 135), and further she ignores his order, "tell, these headstrong women / What duty do they owe their lords and husbands" (5.2.131-32), extending her argument to "Such duty as the subject owes the prince" (5.2.156) and the relation between herself and her husband (5.2.171-76), which Petruchio does not order her to mention. Clearly Pinter knew this long speech of Katherina, because he had appeared in *The Taming of the Shrew* in early 1950's[4] in the role of Hortensio, who listens to Katherina's speech and says to Petruchio, "Now go thy ways, thou hast tam'd a curst shrew" (5.2.189) immediately after Petruchio's "kiss me, Kate." We cannot be sure in what tone he said this line.

    In contrast to Katherina's completely successful disguise, Ruth's disguise as an obedient woman and a prostitute is subtly discernible. For she postpones the date of the contract ("we'll leave it till later" [94]), so Max feels anxious, saying, ". . . she'll do the dirty on us. . . . she'll make use of us" (97). His anxiety is about her ruling the family, replacing him, and overthrowing the patriarchy. It is from this fear of his that he says to her at last, "Kiss me." It is a patriarchal command like that of Petruchio as well as a sexual demand. Though he says, "she won't be . . . adaptable!" (97), she is adaptable, ironically, like the man in Pico's *Oration* who has "the power to transform himself into whatever he chooses" (Wind 191). It is from another self or another fragment of her self that she suddenly calls Teddy "Eddie" as a term of endearment and says, "Don't become a stranger" (96), when she separates from her husband who returns to America. This means she continues in the role of wife to Teddy even if she becomes a mother and a wife to the London family, but it is also a pretence.

Judging from the implications of her actions in the final scene, we cannot help but regard the aspects of her as prostitute, wife and mother as not reality but as disguise or fiction. Here we can apply the second "realism," Bell's X ray "realism," or Dobrez's extreme empiricism, from whose viewpoint Ruth's unified self, or an ideal self embodied in her, could be observed as dispersed, divided and fragmented. As the ideal self of man was divided into the three sons, the ideal self of woman is divided into fragments in Ruth. We might be able to call this kind of self in Ruth the self of the eighteenth century empiricist David Hume. According to Terry Eagleton, "The self for David Hume is a convenient fiction, a bundle of ideas and experiences whose unity we can only hypothesize" (79). Dobrez insists that "Pinter takes empiricism, the apotheosis of the object, to a Humean point," and points out the insubstantiality of Hume's self as does Eagleton, saying "Hume reduces . . . human identity to a collection of sensations" (353). The multiplicity is seen in the self of Ruth, but it is divided, not unified.

From these arguments, in conclusion, through the play we only witness some fragments of the self in each character. No wonder they have inconsistencies. But from another angle, the commonsensical realism, some inconsistencies have a causal relationship, the self seeming to be unified and autonomous. This suggests that just as Shakespeare maintained a double awareness toward the changing of the world view of the Renaissance, Pinter understands the transformation of epistemology caused by the development of modern science. We can affirm *The Homecoming* is one example of his recognition of this.

Notes
1. See Esslin *Pinter* 125-46 on the archetypal approach and Silverstein *Harold Pinter* 76-107 on the Lacanian approach.
2. On the plays acted in by Pinter, see David T. Thompson 127, 128
3. On Katherina's disguise, see Hosokawa 103-25.
4. Pinter appeared many times in *The Taming of the Shrew*, in the role of Hortensio in 1951-2 and late 1953 with Anew McMaster in Ireland, and in the role of Nicholas in February-April 1953 with Donald Wolfit at the King's Theatre, Hammersmith (Thompson 127-78).

5
The "New" Modernity and Doubles in *No Man's Land*

As is well known, Pinter is one of the absurd writers[1] and Dobrez points out the phenomenological characteristic in *No Man's Land*, saying,

> ... the treatment of this film [*The Basement*] returns us to the combination of inward and outward viewpoints characteristic of the phenomenological plays.... After *Old Times* there is a similar return with *No Man's Land* (1975). (362)

No Man's Land is one of Pinter's memory plays which, Christopher Innes says, "build on Eliot's lines, 'Time present and time past / Are both perhaps present in time future.... And all time is unredeemable' from *The Four Quartets*" (154). In the world of the "new" modernity, or the double awareness of modernism, reality lies in the subjective apprehension of the world, which is similar to the phenomenological one. Dobrez says about the drama, "Although the situation of four men ... involves reminiscence in a context of realism, the absence of an objective viewpoint is ... felt, and ... reality takes on expressionist colouring" (362-63). As Esslin points out, "Expressionist drama is full of *Doppelgänger figures* ..." ("Modernist" 534), we can find a theme of doubles in *No Man's Land*, too, which some critics discover in Hirst and Spooner.[2]

In this way, *No Man's Land* betrays the double awareness of realism and subjectivism in modernism, and is permeated by the new mentalities of the "new" modernity of "becoming" and "Time-mind" (Banmer 402). This chapter investigates the nature of the double-relation between Hirst and Spooner, and its meanings in the "new" modernity.

1

The play develops the relation between Hirst and Spooner, seemingly, in a context of realism. Hirst, a literary man, *"precisely dressed"* meets Spooner at a pub, an elderly tramp *"in a very old and shabby suit "* (77), who is "a pintpot attendant in the Bull's Head " according to Briggs (110), and brings him home for a drink. This situation is similar to one at the beginning of *The Caretaker* when Aston brings a seedy man, Davies to his room.

Hirst and Spooner are opposite in some respects. Hirst is "reticent" whereas Spooner speaks with "startling candour" (79). While Hirst lacks "manliness" (94), Spooner is strong ("From this [his mother's hate] I derive my strength" [88]). Spooner says "I am interested in where I am eternally present and active" (82), and "I am a free man" (83). In contrast with him, Hirst is passive, being in "impotence" (95) and drawn to the past. Though he talks about a "memory of the bucolic life," urged on by Spooner, that memory is about the village church whose "beams are hung with garlands, in honour of young women of the parish, reputed to have died virgin" (91) as well as "old men . . . who also died maiden" (92). That past is one which couldn't dispense with absolutes like the church before the revolution of the "new" modernity. Since such a past is gone, his memories are "the quaint little perversions of your life and times" (92), as Spooner points out.

His present situation is like "the death-in-life paralysis" (Gale 220) with absolutes lost. Such a state is manifested by his incessant drinking in Act I. He drinks two shots of vodka after "Cheers" (77) to Spooner who is welcomed, and drinks two more shots of it, hearing his stories of peeping and being a free man (82, 83). After that, he joins Spooner "in a whisky" (84), and further asks him "to pour me another drop of whisky" (89) before Spooner's introduction of himself. He drinks one more shot of whisky, *"with a slight stagger"* (93), before he *"crawls towards the door ... crawls out of the door"* (96) near the middle of Act I. He admits this situation to be chronic, saying "I'd sit here forever, waiting for a stranger to fill up my glass" (107). Though Hirst is taken care of by Foster and Briggs, his secretaries, and he, therefore, should live comfortably, he feels lonely and alienated, for it seems as if he is controlled rather than served by them, like the master ruled by his servant in Pinter's screenplay *The Servant* (1963). We witness Briggs ordering Hirst to "Get up" and "keep on the move," when he leaves the room (114), or we see Foster impatiently directing him to take a walk: "I said it's time for your walking" (139). Guru Charan Behera argues that "they [the secretaries] represent the system that ruthlessly suppresses individualism" (66).

When Spooner says to Hirst, "You've lost your wife of hazel hue.... she will no more come back to you," he feels he lives in a wasteland.

> No man's land ... does not move ... or change ... or grow old ... remains ... forever ... icy ... silent. (96)

No man's land symbolizes this desolate existential situation of the world. The play proceeds in the manner of realism as Spooner offers "myself to you as a friend" and "your boatman" (95) and Foster and Briggs suspect that he invades their house and robs them of their position as secretary ("We're in a position of trust. Don't try to drive a wedge into a happy household" 112).

But the play seems to develop an unrealistic context. Hirst and

Spooner are one man or they are doubles. In other words, they are the split self or mind. If Hirst is a protagonist of the drama, Spooner is his double.

2

Baumer argues that, "By this standard [Time-mind] the new modernity spelled nihilism as well as temporality;"

> . . . living in a world become[*sic*], in the words of the Spanish philosopher Ortega y Gasset, "scandalously provisional," not merely changing, but without the standards or roots. (403)

Further, he describes two parts of the mind of the "new" modernity through Ortega's one as follows:

> The existential part of Ortega's mind rejoiced at the opportunity this situation gave European man to improve and create. But another part was fearful, lest the "revolt" leave European man demoralized, possessed of fabulous power, but not knowing what to do with it, palsied by a sense of loss and insecurity. (403)

In short, the mind of the "new" modernity has two tendencies: free improvisation or creation and being paralyzed or nihilistic.

We can suppose that Ortega's mind is split into Hirst and Spooner. If Ortega's mind is Pinter's, this play can be, as Anthony Suter insists, "a drama of a double character, of dual possibilities in man and the artist, set in a framework which is itself the mind of the artist" (89). But we'd like to regard Hirst as the protagonist of the drama who embodies the whole mind of the "new" modernity at the end, and Spooner as Hirst's part or double, as Katherine H. Burkman argues about the double in Pinter's works: "By portraying the doubles as characters who are independent of the protagonists yet a part of them . . . Pinter offers a vision of life that has both psychological and spiritual dimension" ("Death" 143). In our case, the psychological dimension corresponds to a context of realism, while the spiritual one is related to some traits of the "new" modernity, such as improvisation in the absurd condition.

The possibility that Spooner can be considered as the double of Hirst would be inferred by many similarities common to both men. First of all, they are poets (89, 148). They often use and repeat almost the same words and contents. Hirst's first line in the drama, "As it is?" is followed by Spooner's "As it is, please . . ."(77). When Hirst says "I cannot say," Spooner responds with "It cannot be said" (88). When Spooner says "when we had our cottage . . . we gave our visitors tea, on the lawn," Hirst says, too, "I did the same" (90). They were patrons of the young poets. They are similar as for a family structure and age as both have "grandchildren," "have fathered," and are "of an age" (109).

There are two references or events which would convince us of their identification. One is when Hirst answers "You'd pissed yourself" (88) and "Twenty eight" (89) to Spooner's questions about the cause of his mother's hatred to him and about when his pissing himself was. Spooner affirms Hirst's answers, saying "Quite right" (89). Nobody except himself would be able to answer such personal questions. The other is Spooner's saying: "It was I drowning in your dream" (109) when Hirst asks himself "Who was drowning in my dream?" (108) after he awoke from some oppressing dream. This identification of a drowning man with Spooner in Hirst's dream makes it clear that Spooner is a man in Hirst's mind. He might be a part of Hirst's whole self which lacks or stagnates something lively.

3

Pinter is a typical writer of the "new" modernity of becoming and "Time-mind". He thinks that there are no absolutes, standards and roots in life and the world. "A thing is not necessarily either true or false"; therefore, "it can be both true and false" ("Writing for the Theatre" 11). This idea is one of becoming and changing. As far as time is concerned, he says to Mel Gussow, "I certainly feel more and more that the past is not past, that it never was past. It's present," ". . . previous parts are alive and present," and "I'm more conscious of a kind of ever-present quality in life" (Gussow 38). He affirms the synchronicity of the past and the present, which comes from Bergson's idea of time or "the uninterruptible, indistinguishable flow of time" (Bradbury and McFarlane 431). Bergson's time is a modern one which comes from the denial of time, spatialized or causal, an old idea of time before the revolution of physics in the twentieth century. It is the same as Heidegger's "lived time" (Charles Taylor 463).

    Pinter seems to create the figure of Spooner from these new ideas about truth and time. It is partly for this reason that it is uncertain what he is, and impenetrable whether his sayings are true or false. When he says to Hirst, "I myself can do any graph of experience you wish, to suit your taste or mine" (82), he reveals that he is a restless improviser of some story, whether past or present. One of such improvised stories would be the story about a man of "the Hungarian aristocracy" (86) with "a measure of serenity" (87) whom he met at a pub and whose way of sitting "made me what I am" (87). We can also detect such a fabrication in another story about his picture, "The Whistler" (101) which he says he drew in Amsterdam when he saw a fisherman landing a fish in the canal.

    Though he is an incessant improviser of stories, significantly, his improvising or creation has the constructive effect of stimulating Hirst's stagnated and paralyzed mind or self and activating it. After he boasts of his wife's physical glamour, whose truth is uncertain, he mentions "hazel eyes" scornfully (94), which has a sexual innuendo, from the colour of eyes, hazel, of Hirst's wife, and makes Hirst, "a quiet one," (81), get angry: Hirst "*throws his glass at him*" (94). Then Spooner says, "Things are looking up." He takes, as it were, a role as a stimulus to Hirst's being enlivened. In fact, Hirst starts to change himself or reveal a lacking part or latent part of his self: "Tonight . . . you find me in the last lap of a race. . . . I had long forgotten to run" (94).

The context of realism seems to attribute Hirst's change to his mental breakup caused by heavy drinking. He has so often drunk before he leaves the room once as we saw, and has lost a sense of time ("What day is it? What's the time? Is it still night? " [105]), and forgets Spooner's identity ("Who's that? A friend of yours? " [106]), when he comes back to the room after sleeping for a while, toward the end of Act I. And he describes his incoherent dream in his sleep: "Brightness, through leaves . . . In the bushes. Young lovers . . . The lake. Who was drowning in my dream?" "Theirs is a gap in me. I can't fill it. There's a flood running through me. . . . I'm suffocating. It's a muff. . . . Someone is doing me to death" (108).

From Hirst's description of this dream, we can guess that this scene is not handled in a context of realism such as mental disorder, but as a kind of surrealism or expressionism. "[T]hrough leaves," and "In the bushes" remind us of Spooner who was "a betwixt twig peeper" (80), and "a flood running through me" suggests Spooner's pissing himself at twenty eight. Spooner often uses a sexual pun, as is seen in "buns" (89), "hazel eyes," and now Hirst uses it in "muff." All of them imply female genitals. Though Spooner was drowning in Hirst's dream, we had better say, rather, Spooner coexists in Hirst who narrates the dream. Spooner is Hirst.

What Hirst was dreaming reveals his present existential condition, including his anxiety and insecurity ("Something is depressing me" [106], "someone is doing me to death" [108]), and tells his past remembrance of friends at a picnic. Hirst saw his girl friend or some female classmate in the dream ("She looked up . . . I had never seen anything so beautiful" [108]), and he recalls her again when he talks about his past friends in his photograph album ("When I stood my shadow fell upon her. She looked up" [108]). When he recalls her in this remembrance, her image or the girls' image is good and graceful ("their grace, the ease with which they sit, pour tea" [106]). Hirst, who is demoralized in this new age, misses the past stable world with "A tenderness towards our fellows" ([106]). He says "It [my youth] existed. It was solid, the people in it were solid" (107).

But the girl in his dream discloses another side of her. Her "muff" implies female genitals, and he seems to be "suffocating" with these (108). As Elin Diamond says, "he feels strangled by a woman's 'muff' (slang for female genitals)" (196). She might have had a sexual aspect. If so, the dream reflects Hirst's own subjective or unconscious sexual reality. A sexual side of his self finds itself emerging. His double, Spooner, also already implies female sexual offensiveness in some metaphors from cricket: "Tell me with what speed she swung in the air, with what velocity she came off the wicket" (92). Diamond remarks that Spooner "twists cricket jargon to make obscenely funny suggestions . . ." (196).

This combination of sexuality and sport seems to suggest that sexuality in the play is seen from the viewpoint of life and presentness. Pinter remarks that "The only time I can ever be said to live in the present is when I'm engaged in some physical activity" (Gussow 38). Sex and cricket are both physical activities which give a man a sense of living now. In Act I the past and the present are set apart by either a dream or a remembrance. But when Hirst appears for the second time in Act II, the past and the present mix and coexist.

4

When Hirst reappears in Act II, we see him changed completely. He mistakes Spooner for Charles, an old friend of his at Oxford who was "a gentleman" (136). The realistic interpretation would ascribe this misconception of his to his complete mental breakdown from his intoxication. But when we hear him confess to Charles candidly and triumphantly unlike himself in Act I that he had an affair with Charles's wife, Emily ("That summer she was mine, when you imagined her to be solely yours" [128]), we notice that we are witnessing from this moment the expressionist development of the play in which truth and falsehood or reality and fantasy are uncertain and indistinguishable, and identities cannot be confirmed.

First of all, we are not certain whether Charles is a real person or a fictitious one. Though Spooner is mistaken for Charles, his unsuspicious response to Hirst is unexplainable. Does he know Charles or does he go along with Hirst's fantasies, assuming the role of Charles? When Spooner/Charles, in his turn, blames Hirst for seducing Stella Winstanley, whom Hirst doesn't remember ("Stella who?" [130]), and Spooner/Charles loved ("I was also frightfully fond of Stella" [132]), it is uncertain, too, whether Stella is real or imaginative and whether Spooner/Charles fabricates Hirst's seducing or his reproach is based on the fact, taking it into consideration that Hirst seems to know Bunty who is Stella's brother ("Oh, Bunty. No, I never see her" [131]).

If Hirst is accused based on facts, who is accusing, Charles or Spooner? Does Spooner know the personal relations between Charles, Hirst, Stella and Bunty, and blame Hirst, disguising himself as Charles? Or is Spooner the same man as Charles? Later Spooner blames Hirst for the reason that "you betrayed Stella Winstanley with Emily Spooner, my own wife" (134). Emily was Charles's wife. Hirst himself asks Spooner/ Charles , "who are you?" (136) in the end.

The difficulty of escaping from an intricate maze of identities is predicted symbolically by the impossibility of exiting from Bolsover street in London which Briggs asserts to Spooner in Act I: "Bolsover street was in the middle of an intricate one-way system. It was a one way system easy enough to get into. The only trouble was that, once in, you couldn't get out" (120).

Aside from the credibility of these, Hirst's mistaking of the present Spooner for the past Charles and the following old amatory stories by the two of them show us the mixture of the past and the present or the fabrication of the past by the present, and further the nature of fictitiousness of the world. Anna in *Old Times* (1971), one of Pinter's memory plays, says "There are things I remember which may never have happened but as I recall them so they take place" (28). Thomas P. Adler argues from this view of the past that "Memory can thus become a creative activity, and the remembrance a work of art" (137). Behera goes as far as to argue that "What is expressed and what has happened are all fantasies, projections, enactments" (66) in this play.

But we notice that there is one certain reality that looms up in a series of two people's ambiguous and fantastic dialogues about past memories, which farcically both express Hirst's subconsciousness and remind us of the modern human self, which is "multiple" (Eagleton 66). It is the clear manifestation of another side of Hirst's self which was hidden or latent in him, and embodied through his double, Spooner in Act I. The manner of its appearance is Shakespearian. Lysander in *A Midsummer Night's Dream* (1595-6), who is anointed with an aphrodisiac "love-juice" (3. 2. 37) by Puck in his sleep sees Helena after he awakes and woos her suddenly, betraying Hermia, his true love. His false wooing of her reveals another potentially amorous side of his self, which is called a "hypothetical future" by Edward Berry.[3]

This effect is reflected in Hirst's sudden frank confession of a love affair with Emily when he reappears and takes Spooner for Charles. A realistic interpretation would assert that Hirst' mind has become disoriented not by some supernatural power like "love-juice," but by the influence of too much alcohol. The changed image of Charles, or the image of a sexual man, which arises from his mistaking of the sexual Spooner for the gentle Charles, also might reflect this hidden side of Hirst's self. Charles might be Hirst's double. Charles is "a literary man," "As was I [Hirst] " (128). Hirst asks Charles,"Do you run still?" (128). Hirst was also a runner "who had long forgotten to run" (94). Charles who had "the moral ardour " before (136) now confesses, to Hirst's surprise, that he "had an affair with Arabella" (134) , whom Hirst "was very fond of " (133), and reveals shamelessly that she had "her particular predilection" of "Consuming the male member" (134).

Further Charles slanderously accuses Hirst of seducing Muriel Blackwood, Doreen Busby and Geoffrey Ramsden (134). Hirst, who has been alleged to be lewd, gets angry with him: "This is scandalous!" (135). Hirst, who believes the narrator is Charles, not Spooner, is shocked to know "how the most sensitive and cultivated of men can so easily change, almost overnight, into the bully, the cutpurse, the brigand" (136). This sexually corrupt image of Charles has been born from the mix-up of the two men. But this is a comical caricature of the latent sexual side of Hirst himself reflected in his double, Charles/Spooner.

This is also a Shakespearian reflection from *The Comedy of Errors*. Peoples' mistaking of the twin, Antipholus of Ephesus, for another twin, Antipholus of Syracuse, brings forth an amorous and violent image of Antipholus of Ephesus, which reveals a hypothetical future for him.[4] As for what happens with Hirst's taking of Spooner for Charles, Dobrez argues that "there is a Ionesco multiplication which . . . has the appearance of a farce, if a grim one" (363). In this expressionist situation, Hirst multiplies into the present Spooner and the past Charles, who coexist, and we find him, too, improvising stories no less lively than Charles/Spooner, as we can confirm in his confession of the love affair. His improvisation means he is ready to escape from the death-in-life paralysis in Act I. He absorbs an improvising self and a sexual and vital self from his doubles.

5

Though Hirst begins to change from confronting the past Charles, the past, in the form of Hirst's album, is shown as what stimulates the paralyzed present, as Behera argues: "memory and nostalgia are brought up as illusion to counter the present dullness and decay" (93).

> HIRST. . . . I might even show you my photograph album. . . . You might see faces of others . . . whom you thought long dead, but from whom you will still receive a sidelong glance, if you can face the good ghost. . . . but . . . who knows how they may quicken . . . in their chains, in their glass jars. . . . they wish to respond to your touch . . . . And so I say to you, tender the dead, as you would yourself be tendered, now, in what you would describe as your life. (137)

The past which "may quicken" by "your touch" activates the dull present, as seen in Hirst. If a man wishes for tenderness in life, he must revive "the good ghost" tenderly in his mind.

But as Briggs points out, the "faces of others" are "blank" (137), too. Here we recognize that the play displays the dual traits of the new modernity, both the absurd and the improvisatorial or creative dimensions. The former signifies "the kind of universe men supposedly lived in; devoid of meaning . . . ; lacking being, or essence . . . ; . . . irrational and incomprehensible" (Baumer 414), losing the absolutes. The latter includes the re-creation or construction of life and the world in our minds. Hirst, who was palsied by the absurd condition, has absorbed the latter quality from his double, Spooner or Charles, but the dual traits don't necessarily reconcile in him. Despite his disappointment at his friend's change, he tries to be "patient" with this absurd world, "kind to you" (136), like King Lear,[5] and positively construct a communal companionship with the people around him ("Be sociable. Consort with the society to which you're attached" [143]), while it is true that he feels alienated yet at the same time ("There are places in my heart . . . where no living soul . . . has . . . or can ever . . . trespass" [142]).

In the context of realism, Spooner, who has "fallen on hard times" but whose "will to work has not been eroded" (146, 147), asks Hirst "to consider me for the post [the secretary]," and says, about the post, "I will accept death's challenge on your behalf" (146, 147), or "I would be happy to offer you an evening of your own" in poetry readings (148). But Hirst tries to exclude him, saying "Is there a big fly in here? I hear buzzing" (146). According to Gale, the metaphor of a fly buzzing implies death since "it recalls Emily Dickinson's 'I heard a fly buzz when I died'" (220). It is Spooner that dies. Hirst's disregard of him is, in the context of expressionism, the elimination of his double now that Hirst has absorbed Spooner's element.

But his further refusal of Spooner's long improvisation of a plea for the job (146-49) indicates both the double's extinction and his unstable acquisition of the improvisational element absorbed from Spooner. He replies to Spooner's plea, "Let us change the subject. . . . For the last time"

(149), trying to stop improvising. Foster confirms that Hirst cannot live a creative life anymore, living a mental death: "If the subject is winter, for example, spring will never come" (150). "So that nothing else will happen forever. You'll simply be sitting here forever" (152). This is in opposition to the "new" modernity of becoming and changing. It is a return to the death-in life condition. Briggs and Foster prove to be symbolic of a paralyzed absurd world of the "new" modernity. If so, a condition of being "palsied by a sense of loss and insecurity" (Baumer 403) would last long.

But Hirst changes the subject again, saying "I hear sounds of birds.... I hear them as they must have sounded then, when I was young, although I never heard them then, although they sounded about us then" (152-53). His saying that he can now hear what he cannot before implies the change or growth of Hirst's self whose part was lacking or latent before, and suggests that the recognition of the world is done not by objectivity but by sensibility or subjectivity; in other words, the world is constructed through improvisation.

Thus the play continues to display each of two parts of Ortega's mind referred to above alternately till the end. Again Hirst, just before the close, completely denies the very existence of someone equivalent to Spooner in the play:

> I am walking towards a lake. Someone is following me, through the trees. . . . I say to myself, I saw a body, drowning. But I am mistaken. There is nothing there. . . . (153)

Yet his double, Spooner reminds him of his own earlier nihilistic words in Act I: "No, you are in no man's land. Which never moves . . . never changes . . . never grows older, but which remains forever, icy and silent" (153). This time we hear Hirst answer to him, "I'll drink to that." Though this last reply is elusive and ambiguous, we can recognize that his last situation lies in both the affirmation and the denial of no man's land. It can be said that the play ends with Hirst suspended in the stasis between flickering life and mental death. "*He drinks*" (153) between a bringer of life or creation, Spooner and a pair of mediums for stagnation, Briggs and Foster when the curtain closes. As Burkman puts it, the play "provides us with insight into the dynamics of modern man's struggle with life and his retreat from living it fully" ("Death" 143).

Notes
1. See Esslin *Theatre* 234-64.
2. See A. Suter and Burkman "Death".
3. About Lysander's sudden exchange of lovers, Berry says, "The characters enact their potential for tragedy in actions that are re-creative, as dream or play may be in actual life," and call their potential for change "hypothetical future" (153).
4. On the "hypothetical future" in *The Comedy of Errors*, see note 2 in chapter 3.
5. In *King Lear* "the absolute has ceased to exist. It has been replaced by the absurdity of the human situation," (108) as Jan Kott says. Kott sees it as an absurd and grotesque drama. King Lear who has recognized the absurdity of the world, shut out from his daughters' castles into the stormy wilderness, remarks "I will be the pattern of all patience" (3. 2. 35) and begins to show his kindness to the people, saying to Kent who recommends him to enter a hovel, "Prithee, go in thyself, seek thine own ease" (3. 4. 23). In this regard, Jay L. Halio notes that "Lear has begun to consider others first" (182).

6
The Meaning of Rebecca's Disguise as a Dispossessed Mother in *Ashes to Ashes*

In the last scene of Pinter's political play *Ashes to Ashes* (1996), which Pinter says "*is* about the images of Nazi Germany" ("Writing, Politics" 246), Rebecca narrates to Devlin one of the past incidents she witnessed in which a woman was walking to the station, "carrying a baby in her arms" (71). In her narrating of the woman's movement and behavior, she suddenly changes the pronoun of the woman she describes from "she" to "I." Many critics agree that Rebecca here identifies herself with the woman, a clear victim of the Holocaust.

> REBECCA. *She* listened to the baby's heartbeat. The baby's heart was beating.
> . . . .
> *I* held her to me. She was breathing. Her heart was beating.
> (73 italics mine)

Though Rebecca "took my baby and wrapped it in my shawl," "made it into a bundle," and "held it under my left arm" (77), she was dispossessed of her baby by a soldier at the station as "the baby cried out" (79). While some critics call this identification of hers Rebecca's empathetic identification,[1] Jessica Prinz says "it is an instance of actual transformation" (97-98), or as Elizabeth Angel-Perez argues, "Rebecca's individual personality dissolves into otherness"(156). However we'd like to see it as a kind of "disguise."

This disguise is defined as "the substitution, overlaying or metamorphosis of dramatic identity, whereby one character sustains two roles" (Bradbrook, "Shakespeare" 160). Here Rebecca sustains two identities, one as a woman who narrates the Holocaust, the other as a victim of it. This pattern of her disguise reminds us of that in the sixteenth century humanist drama. As Kent Cartwright puts it,

> A fascinating element of humanist dramaturgy . . . is its melding of . . . two versions of the individual, one as a private and unique identity, the other communal and shared. A recurrent strategy of humanist dramaturgy, from *Wit and Science* to . . . *Hamlet*, is to posit a character as a separate self and then to reveal progressively his or her shared identity with others. (65)

Humanist drama is apt to develop a character in the fusion of a private identity and a communal and shared identity, and disguise often works to meld them.[2] In Rebecca's disguise, we notice Echo repeat every word of Rebecca after her disguising herself as a dispossessed mother,

```
REBECCA.   They took us to the trains
ECHO.      the trains            (75)

REBECCA.   They were taking away the babies away.
ECHO.      the babies away       (77)
```

Echo's repetition convinces us that her second identity represents a communal and shared one. Rebecca as dispossessed mother shares this identity with the victims of atrocity. Mireia Aragay calls this identity "a shared subjectivity in pain" (254) while Angel-Perez regards it as "collective character, the paragon of all the mothers of the war, a metonymical representative of all the group" (156).

In John Redford's *Wit and Science* (c.1530-47), a humanist drama, Wit lets himself be disguised as Ignorance in his sleep, the attributes such as motley coat and hood being conferred on him by Idleness (570.1, 583.1), and changes his behavior into those of Ignorance afterwards ("Now are ye . . . / Cunjur'd from Wit unto a starke foole" 589-91). He has had a shared identity with Ignorance, and Wit, at the end, recognizes in the mirror his doubleness with him (800-16), attaining self-discovery as usual in humanist dramaturgy (Cartwright 65). In the case of *Ashes to Ashes*, Rebecca as private identity is a friend of a Nazi and a woman who narrates the atrocity to Devlin, her present lover or husband. She is, in this position, at first indifferent to the Nazi atrocity or rather an accomplice of it, but by her disguise she learns to share a communal identity with all the victims of the Holocaust.

Though the function of disguise is common in both plays, its effects and implications seem to be very different. In this chapter we attempt to clarify the meaning of Rebecca's disguise and its implications in relation to the play's combination of two themes of atrocity and the self behind it. Christopher Wixton points out these two themes, too, but from a different angle from ours, saying "While *Ashes to Ashes* invokes the trauma of human suffering and atrocities, it also suffers from the trauma of fractured subjectivity" (16).

Pinter represents some of his characters in a few plays up until *No Man's Land* from the perspective of a modernist double awareness, using some kind of disguise. Though Teddy, Lenny and Joey in *The Homecoming* seem to have a unified self, Esslin says, "Lenny and Joey are complementary. . . . these two could be seen as different aspects of one personality" (*Pinter* 142). This is also true of Hirst and Spooner in *No*

Man's Land. Seemingly each has a unified self, but they seem to be each other's double. Rebecca's disguise has a relation to this "double awareness," too. Before examining this in detail, we need to see in what circumstances she is situated in the play.

1

As is known well, Pinter wrote this play influenced by Gitta Sereny's biography of Albert Speer "who was Hitler's favourite architect, Minister for Armaments and Munitions from 1942" (Billington 374). Rebecca's ex-lover is completely surrounded by an atmosphere of Nazism or fascism. According to Lunn, Adorno and Horkheimer argue that "barbarism resurfaces in the twentieth century through the return of a 'nature' which had been thwarted and brutalized by a technocratic civilization" (239), and they "suggested a theory of 'fascism' as the 'return of the repressed'" (239). This theory seems to be revealed in the drama from the viewpoint of eroticism. We can confirm it in Rebecca's first reference to her ex-lover at the start of the play:

> REBECCA. . . . he would stand over me and clench his fist. And then he'd put his other hand on my neck and grip it and bring my head towards him. His fist . . . grazed my mouth. And he'd say, 'Kiss my fist.'
> DEVLIN.   And did you?
> REBECCA. Oh yes. I kissed his fist. (3)

After her former lover forced her to kiss his fist, he "put a little . . . pressure . . . on my throat. . . . So that my head started to go back, gently but truly" (7). To Devlin's following questions, "And your body? Where did your body go?" "So your legs were opening?" she answers to each,

"My body went back, slowly but truly," "Yes" (7). As Prinz points out, these behaviours suggest "a sado-masochistic relationship" between the man and her (98). What this erotic episode implies definitely is that Rebecca's former lover was a fascist, revealing his sexuality barbarically, though it takes on the appearance of a traditional bourgeois love triangle (Angel-Perez 145). Devlin, her supposed husband or lover who listens to her narration of her past love affair and asks about her lover persistently, wants to dig out and own his lover's past as do Deeley in *Old Times* (1970) and Jerry in *Betrayal* (1978) . We might have an objection to this reading of Rebecca's victimhood by Nazism on the ground that as Rebecca is in her 40's, when the play takes place in 1996, she would be too young to experience the Holocaust, which her former lover evokes as Angel-Perez points out (149). But Pinter uses the poetics of "new" modernity in which the traditional entire space-time continuum is collapsed (Prinz 99), and two temporalities, i.e., "the immediate past" or "the private time of Rebecca" and "the historical time" coexist (Angel-Perez 149). As Francis Gillen puts it, in this play "we enter history at a particular place—a country house in England—at a particular time—the present—but we are at the same time in Buchenwald, the mass graves in Bosnia, anywhere in time and place where police sirens are heard" (91) and an atrocity occurs. "The past Rebecca digs out for us is a past of a universal type" (Angel-Perez 150) while Devlin evokes the past topically or realistically. This is what Pinter implies when he says,

> . . . what happens in my plays could happen anywhere, at any time, in any place, although the events may seem unfamiliar at first glance. . . . what goes on in my plays is realistic, but what I'm doing is not realism. ("Writing for Myself" 11)

He testifies to his "double awareness" here.

The image of the Nazi in Rebecca's former lover is intensified by her later episodes according to which he once took her to "a kind of factory"(23) and there "he ran a really tight ship"(25) or "He used to go to the local railway station . . . and tear all the babies from the arms of their screaming mothers" (27). And this image is also supported by the fact that his factory has an actual model, which is a secret labor camp called Dora which Albert Speer visited in 1943 (Sereny 404). As the prisoners there "ripped off their prisoners' caps" when Speer "walked past these men" at Dora (405), so in the play, Rebecca explains,

> They were all wearing caps . . . the workpeople . . . soft caps . . . and they took them off when he came in, leading me, when he led me down the alleys between the rows of workpeople. (23)

And when Rebecca says, "I wanted to go to the bathroom. But I simply couldn't find it. . . . I'm sure they had one"(27), it reflects what Speer witnessed as to the sanitary provisions at Dora in 1943,

> No heat, no ventilation, not the smallest pail to wash in. . . . The latrines were barrels cut in half with planks laid across. They stood at each exit from the rows of sleeping cubicles. (Sereny 405)

"Bathroom" was "barrels" which "stood at each exit."

2

What is implied about Rebecca herself from her episodes of his Nazi background? To know that, we need to observe her responses when the man makes a sexual command to her with his order, "Kiss my fist." She, far from resisting it, not only submits to it as we saw above, but also says , "Put your hand round my throat" (3) and demands his sadistic attack to put a pressure on her throat. This fact in her narration suggests she is an accomplice of Nazism or fascism. Against Devlin's insisting that the man "tried to murder you" (43) by his pressure on her throat, she defends him, saying, "He felt compassion for me. He adored me" (45). Remembering his words at his factory, "they had such great respect for him" (25), as they were doffing their caps to him, she affirms indifferently, "They had total faith in him. They respected his . . . purity, his . . . conviction" (25). Such complicity of and indifference to atrocity as these are discerned in her other narrated episodes, too. In an episode where a police siren is heard, she says to Devlin suddenly, "we heard a couple of minutes ago" (29), and says, "I hate losing it. I hate somebody else possessing it. I want it to be mine, all the time. It's such a beautiful sound" (31), forgetting the siren menacing the innocent, and betraying her position on the side of power. These relations of hers to atrocity are symbolized by her story about a pen which "rolled right off, onto the carpet" (35). When she calls it "this perfectly innocent pen" (35), Devlin says, "You can't sit there and say things like that" (37) because "You don't know . . . what other people have been doing with it" (35), and points out her stance of indifference.

Though she introduces such some episodes as seen above, they are neither directly connected, consistent, nor causal but haphazard. This is suggested by the frequent repetition of a phrase "By the way" before narrating them: "By the way, there's something I've been dying to tell you" (33). This inconsistency in her words reveals to us the state of her own self. In order to see it, we might compare her manner of speech and Devlin's, which might reflect their positions in the world. In sharp contrast with her incoherent manner of speech, Devlin's way of speech is logical or causal. It is exemplified in a scene where, irritated at her enigmatic description of her former lover and their love affair, Devlin asks Rebecca about them minutely:

> DEVLIN. There are so many things I don't know. (11)

> DEVLIN. Physically. I mean, what did he actually look like? . . . Length, breadth . . .[. . .] I just want, well, I need . . . to have a clearer idea of him . . . (13)

> DEVLIN. I mean when did all this happen exactly? . . . Was it before you knew me or after you knew me? (33)

Such a feature of his speech reminds us of the traditional realism of cause and effect principles, which implies the "old" modernity and points out a unified self in him associated with the nineteenth century phallic discourse. As he is such a traditional man, he gets angry at Rebecca's suggestion that "God is sinking into a quicksand . . . " (39).

> DEVLIN. That's what I would call a truly disgusting perception. . . . Be careful how you talk about God. . . . If you let him go he won't come back. . . .You know what it'll be like, such a vacuum? It'll be like England playing Brazil at Wembley and not a soul in the stadium. . . . If you turn away from God it means that the great and noble game of soccer will fall into permanent oblivion. . . . Absence. Stalemate. Paralysis. (39-41)

Thus the "old" modernity, part of Pinter's double awareness is revealed in his description of the necessity of the Absolute. But his unified self proves to be an illusion at the end of the drama by his assuming Rebecca's ex-lover's fascist identity. When Rebecca suddenly starts to disguise herself as a victim of the atrocity, as mentioned above,

> *Devlin goes to her. He stands over her and looks down at her. He clenches his fist and holds it in front of her face. . . . He brings her head towards his fist. His fist touches her mouth.*
> DEVLIN. Kiss my fist.   (73-75)

Devlin mimics the same sexual behaviors that her lover took at the start of the play. A kind of disguise seen here shows the division of his unified self or rather the illusoriness of his unified self, but yet the fact that he assumes a sadistic Nazi stance implies that he pursues the "old" modernity illusively or dogmatically, which the Enlightenment has developed. The Enlightenment has a close relation to such eroticism as sadomasochism about which Horkheimer and Adorno, in their book *Dialectic of Enlightenment* (1944), argue that "implicit in the beginning of the Enlightenment . . . was the synthesis of reason, domination, and myth that was revealed in all its truth in de Sade's orgies . . . and then put into practice in Auschwitz" (Herf 233-34).[3] Devlin, logical and authoritative ("You could have treated me like a priest" [45]), shouts, "I'm in the dark. I need light" (11), which recalls literally Enlightenment (from 'en-lighten'), darkened by the uncertain identity of Rebecca's lover and jealous of his sadistic attack on her. Devlin is clearly a descendant of the Enlightenment, and the Nazi's sadism or fascism is one effect from a technocratic civilization which comes from the Enlightenment. The fascist, Rebecca's former lover reappears in Devlin. All of these facts suggest that "the twentieth century world is one of organized cruelty on a large scale" (Esslin, "Harold Pinter's Theatre" 30). Pinter's play warns us of this danger latent in the world of the "new" modernity.

3

The division or fragmenting of the self seen in Devlin is the state of Rebecca's own self from the start. Despite Devlin's wish, they live in the world of "Paralysis" in God's "Absence," a dark reality of the "new" modernity, which is characterized by Heidegger's existential philosophy, *Sein and Zeit*, in which "Heidegger's nazism was latent" (Herf 112). And as Heidegger "could find a way out through identification with a national collective subject" (112) so Devlin, who has lost the Absolute, has found it through his identification with that Nazi, a national collective subject, instead of God in the "old" modernity.

Baumer says that "the new modernity spelled nihilism as well as temporality," and that "living in a world become . . . 'scandalously provisional,' not merely changing, but without standards or roots" (403). Provisional living can produce not consistency but multiplicity in a man, because it gives a man the moment "to improvise" (403).

Clearly Rebecca's random way of narrating or improvising some enigmatic episodes, her varied relations to atrocity, her fusion of the past and the present, and her final assuming of disguise have a close relation to this provisional living. The twentieth century world of the "new" modernity brings nihilism, a "sense of loss" which the three words [i.e. the Absurd, anxiety, and alienation] attest (Baumer 414). In the waste land of the "new" modernity, Rebecca lives multiple lives in contrast with Devlin's illusory absolutist living like the Nazi's.

This is the reason why, as Prinz puts it, "Rebecca occupies different and contradictory subject-positions in the play" (98). She occupies a position of a witness of atrocity, too.

> REBECCA. The guides . . . were ushering all these people across the beach. . . . I saw all these people walk into the sea. The tide covered them slowly. (49)

Rebecca witnessed from the window in the house of Dorset an atrocity in which guides forced "a whole crowd of people" (48-49) to be drowned. She also saw her lover "tear all the babies from the arms of their screaming mothers" (53). And at the end she occupies the position of victim of atrocity in her disguise by handing over "the bundle" (81) of her baby at the station. Prinz argues further that these "multiple subject-positions which she occupies may be an expression of the fact that she is a postmodern subject—decentered, untotalized, multiple, complex" (98).

4

It is true that the state of the self in her is untotalized, multiple, but it seems that it surpasses postmodernism. Here we need to notice what Eagleton says in his recent criticism of postmodernism. He argues that the fault of the postmodern idea of the self is its denial of an element of "self-determination" (89): "What is omitted from this picture [postmodernism] is the fact that human beings are determined precisely in a way which allows them a degree of self-determination" (89), and he further contends that "the humanist notion of the self-determining agent, and the postmodern conception of the multiple subject, are not finally at odds" (66). According to him, "The old 'liberal humanist' self . . . was able to transform the world" (91).

> If there are no such subjects [autonomous subjects] around, all the vital questions over which classical political philosophy has agonized—your rights against mine, my struggle for emancipation

against yours—can simply be dissolved away. (90)

It is from the charge of political quietism, "pernicious ethico-political nature of postmodernism" (Aragay 251) that he argues thus. Aragay says,

> According to Eagleton, the postmodernist positing of the discoherent, isolated subject forecloses the possibility of any truly productive, transformative kind of action, while the enshrining of discursivity implies that neither reality nor discourses about reality nor the subject itself can be submitted to any significant critical discussion—they are all discursively constituted and there is, consequently, no 'outside.' On the basis of this, the possibility of resistance is effectively denied . (252)

We'd like to see this kind of self-determining self in Rebecca's disguise. We can discover this self emerging when this new Rebecca shows her determined resistance to the new fascist's two sexual demands by making no response. As was seen above, Devlin appears as a new Nazi in front of Rebecca who disguises herself as a dispossessed mother, and reenacts the old Nazi's sexual words and behaviors. This time, unlike before, "*She does not move* " to his demand, "Kiss my fist," and "*She does not speak or move*" again even to the second sadistic demand by Devlin, "Say 'Put your hand round my throat'" (75), whose behavior last time she herself demanded to her Nazi lover. Her resistance is implied in her complete disregard of him. And after this, as seen above, Echo repeats the words of Rebecca / dispossessed mother, revealing that she has assumed a social shared identity with all the victims of atrocity.

It is noteworthy here that before this resistance, the play develops her awareness of complicity in atrocity. Her guilt is exposed in an episode of mental elephantiasis. In a condition of this illness, she says,

> REBECCA. . . . when you spill an ounce of gravy . . . it immediately expands and becomes a vast sea of gravy. . . . and you suffocate in a voluminous sea of gravy. (51)

The words of "an ounce of gravy" and "a voluminous sea of gravy" remind us of those of Macbeth after his murder of Duncan :[4]

> MACBETH. Will all great Neptune's ocean wash this blood
> Clean from my hand? No, this my hand will rather
> The multitudinous seas incarnadine. . . .   (*Macbeth* 2. 2. 59-61)

The parallels between both "this blood" and "an ounce of gravy," and "The multitudinous seas" and "a voluminous sea of gravy" implies that as Macbeth feels his guilt strongly, so Rebecca does her guilt. Her sense of guilt is disclosed in her following words,

> You are not the *victim* of it. You are the cause of it. Because it was you who spilt the gravy in the first place, it was you who handed over the bundle. (51)

5

Her last resistance in disguise is, thus, closely connected with her sense of guilt, and on the other hand, her empathetic identification with all the victims of atrocity in her disguise works as a metaphor of audience's engagement with this Rebecca. Pinter expects us in the end to identify with this resistant Rebecca. Gillen agrees with this idea, saying "We, as audience participating in the living ritual of theatre, to the extent that . . .

we identify imaginatively with Rebecca . . . discover with Rebecca that power (to reshape ourselves) in ourselves" (91). On this point, the play is similar to humanist drama because humanist drama is premised on "their [spectators'] engagement with the protagonist's self-discovery" (Cartwright 49). From such points as this social shared identity, a kind of self-determining self coupled with her resistance all of which are born in her disguise, we can assert that her 'self' surpasses the postmodern self, which is only multiple.

But the self in her is not a unified one as argued above. This is reconfirmed by her denial of the existence of her baby before the curtain falls. When a woman "said what happened to your baby" (83) as her train arrives, she and Echo reply,

>   REBECCA. I don't have a baby
>   ECHO.   a baby
>   REBECCA. I don't know of any baby
>   ECHO.   of any baby
>   *Pause*
>   REBECCA. I don't know of any baby
>   *Long silence*
>   BLACKOUT   (83-85)

About her denial, Burkman says, "Rebecca denies her feeling of guilt, which is too awful to face. . . . she can't fully face her own sense of complicity in the holocaust" ("Harold" 93). But we can consider a series of denials as the proof that the self in her is both multiple like the postmodern one and the self-determining one. As for the former, no repetition by Echo of her last denial will prove that she speaks as a private identity and displays one aspect of the incoherent self. It is true that in "this post-Heisenbergian time" (104) as Prinz says, "those who allow atrocity to continue may become its victims" (103), but remembering Rebecca now speaks as a communal identity, too, because Echo repeats her first and second denials, we can also guess that her denial implies that people including her decide to occupy other positions of non-victim and non-victimizer. And Pinter expects us to become like this Rebecca, too, through our empathetic identification with her. Gillen says,

> Like Shakespeare's *Tempest* . . . *Ashes to Ashes* is, besides all else, a play about play, about the ability of art to transform us into something strange . . . only to re-emerge more fully, universally human than before. (97)

Disguise seen in Rebecca symbolizes this ability to make us reemerge fully human beyond postmodernism, too. As the title of the drama, *Ashes to Ashes* and the reappearance of a new fascist suggest, atrocity or tyranny cycles and is repeated in the world throughout history. Pinter says,

> . . . it's not simply the Nazis that I'm talking about in *Ashes to Ashes*. . . . what we call our democracies have subscribed to these repressive, cynical and indifferent acts of murder. ("Writing, Politics" 247).

Pinter asks us, "If you are a democracy and you help people of other countries murder their own citizens, then what are you doing?" ("Writing, Politics" 247-48). [5]

As Pinter so often played in Shakespeare's dramas in his youth, he well knew the "Tudor theatre's ability to engage spectatorial feelings and emotions" (Cartwright 2), an effect of disguise to produce a communal and shared identity, and a metatheatrical power of disguise to transform audience. He, as it were, modernized this theatrical tradition in the play. In this political play Pinter urges, through Rebecca's disguise, our recognition of the importance of resisting any type of tyranny beyond the political quietism of postmodernism, allowing us a postmodern, indeterminate and sometimes contradictory multiplicity.

Notes
1. See Gillen 91; Silverstein "Talking" 82; and "Harold" 93.
2. About Neronis's disguise as a boy in *Clyomon and Clamydes* (c. 1570), Cartwright argues: "disguise allows Neronis to explore and fulfill a 'masculine' aspect of her character otherwise partially suppressed. She demonstrates, as well, the female secret identity, occurring in early humanist drama . . ." (162-63). She combines private female shamefacedness and male courage shared with knights in her disguise, saying "why dost thou not express thy love, to him . . . ? / Because shamefastnesse and womanhood, bids us not seek to men" (ll.1020-21) while saying "The sword of this my loving knight, behold I here do take, / Of this my wofull corps alas, a finall end to make" (ll.1542-43).
3. While Herf argues "The Enlightenment's true face of calculation and domination was evident in de Sade's highly organized tortures and orgies" (9), Pinter says "it [the Holocaust] was so calculated, deliberate and precise" ("Writing, Politics" 247), suggesting its debt to the Enlightenment. However Herf argues that Nazi ideology's debt to it is in its being receptive to "the most obvious manifestation of means-ends rationality, that is, modern technology" (Herf 1).
4. Pinter knew *Macbeth* well because he had played the title role at Hackney Downs Grammar School in 1947; the role of Macduff in the tour of Ireland with the Anew McMaster repertory company, 1951-2 and late 1953; and the role of Second Murderer with the Donald Wolfit Company at the King's Theatre, Hammersmith, Feb-April 1953. (Billington 13; Thompson 127-28)
5. Pinter, here, blames democratic countries such as the United States, Great Britain, and France for selling arms to countries by whose military dictatorship numerous innocent citizens were tortured and killed. In particular, he condemns the US for having "supported, subsidized and in a

number of cases, engendered every right-wing military dictatorship in the world since 1945" as in "Guatemala, Indonesia, Chile, Greece, Uruguay, the Philippines, Brazil, Paraguay, Haiti, Turkey, El Salvador," and Nicaragua where "Hundreds of thousands of people have been murdered by these regimes . . ." ("Open Letter" 255).

7
One for the Road, Party Time, Celebration and Power's Invisibility: From Shakespearian Disguise to Postmodern Subject

About Pinter's later plays Varun Begley argues that they "explore . . . convergences of horror and civility," and points out "the proximity of civility and barbarism" (162) in plays such as *One for the Road* (1984) and *Party Time* (1991). Though he doesn't refer to Pinter's last full-length play *Celebration* (1999), it would be added to such plays, too. Begley has discovered such convergences in Alain Resnais's Holocaust documentary *Night and Fog* (1955). He describes the film as follows:

> [It] begins with the exterior of a comfortable villa, home to a Nazi commandant. The narrator reports that the residence was located near one of the concentration camps. Subsequently three snapshots depict the wives of various commandants. One poses in the parlour, smiling, with a group of well-dressed visitors. Another sits beside her husband, a contented dog in her lap. The banality of these images is somehow intolerable. They evoke real but macabre domestic dramas performed in the shadows of the camps. (162)

The problem of the nearness of civility and barbarism or villainy is pregnant with a variety of themes ideologically, politically and artistically when Pinter's three plays are investigated. This problem has a close relationship to the theme of the modes of power in Western history. It is necessarily linked with the theme of the true nature of a ruler. This consideration goes back as early as the Shakespearian age and through the

Enlightenment. The theme of disguise comes to be involved when we consider rulers in Shakespeare. And the examination of the modes of disguise in power leads us to reflect on the problem of the self or the subject around power.

When we put in temporal order *One for the Road*, clearly a political drama, and *Party Time*, and *Celebration*, seemingly bourgeoisie dramas, or civil ones, and look at them from these viewpoints, each of the latter two plays seems to be a work developed or transformed from the previous play in relation to power, disguise, and the self or subject. The most conspicuous feature in them is that the proximity of civility and barbarism recognized explicitly in *One for the Road* becomes less visible in *Party Time*, and least visible in *Celebration*; in other words, power becomes more and more invisible while civility comes to be foregrounded more and more. At the same time, the visible connection of an individual to power tends to be blurred and to disappear in the latter two plays, whereas power converges on one individual in *One for the Road*.

The theme of the proximity of civility and wickedness in power is a very old one. Machiavelli, the Renaissance philosopher, says that "a prince may not have all the admirable qualities . . . but it is very necessary that he should seem to have them" (48). Here he teaches Renaissance rulers the power of disguise. Though Shakespeare often represents a ruler's disguise, as in *Henry V* (1568-9) and *Measure for Measure* (1604-5),[1] the tradition seems to be reflected somewhat in *One for the Road*. This last chapter reviews these problems or power's modes, disguise in power, and the self or subject in relation to power in Pinter's three later plays, considering some historical background such as thought and theatre, and Pinter's literary aesthetic and his later political life.

1

Since the mid-1980s Pinter's work "has become openly, ostensibly political as opposed to his earlier, more metaphorical explorations of power games" (Aragay 246). *One for the Road* is the first full-length work among such political plays. In the play Nicolas, a high-level bureaucrat, questions the political dissident Victor, his wife Gila and his son Nicky in a detention facility. Though the setting is unspecific as is usual in Pinter, the description of his interrogations is realistic. Nicolas's questioning of Victor at the outset starts with polite frankness:

> Hello! Good morning. How are you? Let's not beat about the bush. Anything but that. *D'accord*? You're a civilized man, So am I. Sit down. (223)

He treats Nicolas as an intellectual ("You're a man of the highest intelligence" [224]), and shows his civility to such a highbrow, saying, "So [a civilized man] am I," or "I am [a religious man]" (224). But his subsequent civil phraseology such as "There is only one obligation. *To be honest*" (230) is opposed to his later ominous and sexual locutions which are "reminders of the ineluctable suffering that rhetorical civility disguises" (Begley 176). He says to Nicolas that he loves the death of others ("Do you love the death of others as much as I do?" [229]). "Does she fuck?" (230) he asks him about his wife, and says, "Your wife and I had a very nice chat. . . . She's probably menstruating" (231). It is clear that these uncivil words refer to killing and rape. Though his speeches don't describe torture directly but focus on its periphery digressively during the play, they imply that violence is done to political dissidents in the detention facility offstage, and that he is closely concerned in it. We can suspect from Nicolas's speeches that he himself adopts the Shakespearian ruler's disguise at the same time as power here hides or disguises cruelty or barbarism.

There are two archetypes in Shakespearian disguise. They are "the disguise of the serpent and the disguise of the Incarnation" (Bradbrook, "Shakespeare" 161). As for rulers, the former is reflected in Machiavellian rulers in whom appearance and reality are different in their sly and evil use of power, hiding cruelty behind civility. The latter is reflected in "the disguised rulers (God's vicegerents), who wander among their subjects . . . in the end distributing rewards and punishments in a judgment scene" (162). Nicolas mentions both types of disguise as to his identity in a dialogue with Victor.

> You probably think I'm part of a predictable, formal, long-established pattern; i.e. I chat away, friendly, insouciant, I open the batting, as it were, in a light-hearted, even carefree manner, while another waits in the wings, silent, introspective, coiled like a puma. No, no. It's not quite like that. I run the place. God speaks through me. . . . Everyman respects me here. (224-25)

Here he surmises that Victor suspects Nicolas to be assuming the disguise of the serpent by which he plays the role of a civil and "friendly" man while playing that of a savage one like a "puma." But he denies such Machiavellian disguise in himself, and suggests that he assumes "heavenly disguise" (Bradbrook, "Shakespeare" 162), by which he takes on the role of God's vicegerent and runs the facility justly. Though he says as a heavenly disguiser, "Everyone else knows the voice of God speaks through me" (227), he soon discloses that he is not a supreme ruler, but a middle-manager of power. There is "the man who runs this country . . ." (230) above him, and who said, "Nic, if you ever come across anyone whom you have good reason to believe is getting on my tits, tell them . . . honesty is the best policy" (231), euphemistically ordering him to torture the dissidents if they resist. Nicolas is much moved when this unidentified ruler makes a patriotic speech to the public.

> NICOLAS. I have never been more moved, in the whole of my life, as when . . . the man who runs this country announced to the country: We are all patriots, we are as one, we all share a common heritage. . . . I feel a link. . . . I share a commonwealth of interest. I am not alone. (232)

According to Silverstein, here "Nicolas's articulated sense of shared identity enacts . . . the kind of abdication of 'self' that it describes. . . . his voice dissolves into the monolithic Voice of state power" ("*One*" 428). Far from being either a Machiavellian disguised ruler, or God's vicegerent in disguise, he "becomes a 'mouthpiece' for a Power that always exceeds him" ("*One*" 429). To say from the viewpoint of the motif of disguise in drama, his disguise corresponds to Lloyd Davis's idea. As referred to above, Davis argues that the "motif of disguise suggests that personal identity is not conceived as essentially or originally present" (4). His definition of disguise, a manipulation of at least two identities, points out the fictitiousness or fracture of the self or subject in both modernist and postmodernist senses. Furthermore, Nicolas is not only an ostensible performer of serpent or God, but also a "*metteur en scène*" (Begley 176). About his performance and producing, Begley says all of his speeches and behaviours "conspire to render the interrogation as spectacle" (177) and argues that his psychic condition resembles "hysterical psychosis, which is marked by the patient's tendency to perform" (177), seeing him, one of "Pinter's modernist thugs" (164), as a "post-Freudian subject" (172). Aside from Nicolas's pathology, his self is not certainly essential, but he is merely an instrument of power. Of course, he is responsible for torture offstage, letting his soldiers rape Gila ("Have they been raping you?" [243]), and ordering them to kill Nicolas's son Nicky ("Your son? Oh, don't worry about him. He was a little prick" [247]), but he is only subject to the supreme authorities invisible onstage.

2

Power's invisibility began in the Enlightenment era. It is embodied in Jeremy Bentham's invention, the Panopticon, in whose "peripheric ring, one [prisoner] is totally seen, without ever seeing; in the central tower, one [warder] sees everything without ever being seen" (Foucault 202). This means that power becomes invisible, in other words, hidden or disguised. We can see the change of modes of power historically here. The mode of power changes, in the eighteenth century, from power on display to disciplinary power which has continued till today. Foucault says,

> Traditionally, power was what was seen, what was shown, and what was manifested and, paradoxically, found the principle of its force in the movement by which it deployed that force. . . . Disciplinary power, on the other hand, is exercised through its invisibility; . . . In it the 'subjects' were presented as 'objects' to the observation of a power that was manifested only by its gaze. (187-88)

The power on display appears in the coronation ceremony, the royal entry and the public executions in the Shakespearian era. Shakespeare represents such power in the distribution of justice and mercy by a disguised ruler, the Duke Vincentio who disguises himself as a monk in *Measure for Measure*. The latter disciplinary power could also be seen in Shakespeare's Prospero before the appearance of the Panopticon.[2] Prospero in *The Tempest* (1611-2) is a ruler disguised as a "sorcerer" (3.2.41) with a "magic garment" (1.2.24) on. He exercises his power without being seen by anybody, using as his agent a literally invisible airy spirit, Ariel ("PROSPERO *and* ARIEL *remain, invisible*" 4. 1. 193. 1). How disciplinary his power is witnessed in Prospero's training Caliban, who is an "Abhorred slave, / which any print of goodness will not take, / Being capable of all ill!" (1. 2. 353-55). Prospero, who has failed to train him says, "A devil, a born devil, on whose nature / Nurture can never stick; on whom my pains, / Humanely taken . . ." (4. 1. 188-90). But Caliban who "wouldst gabble like / A thing most brutish" (1. 2. 358-59) gets angry with such power of his for forcing him to learn his language ("The red plague rid you / For learning me your language!" 1. 2. 366-67). Complaining that "This island's mine, by Sycorax my mother, / Which thou tak'st from me" (1. 2. 333-34), Caliban reveals that such a seeming civil power hides violence.

The same situation is seen in Pinter's *Mountain Language* (1988) where "mountain people" who speak the forbidden "mountain language" (255) are disciplined so that they speak "the language of the capital" (258). Though power is visible on the stage in this play, showing the elderly woman's "thumb is going to come off" (253) by the attack of a torturer's dog, this modern power, it can be said, belongs to a type of invisible power in which only civility is visible, hiding barbarity or violence. It would be *Party Time* that represents such power most typically.

3

In *Party Time*, the violence of power is hidden behind civility. It exists offstage. On the stage a group of bourgeois gather at the flat of Gavin, who holds a cocktail party. One of their topics is a new club of "real class" (283) available only for the members in which "you play a game of tennis, you have a beautiful swim, they've got a bar . . ." (281-82). Gavin is encouraged to join the exercise club as the "cannelloni is brilliant," and they "even do chopped liver" (286). In another corner, Charlotte listens to Liz's anger and envy of her lover's affairs with a young girl. Old people, Gavin and Melissa, talk about small animals ("squirrels" 297) and birds ("hawks," "eagles" 298) in the country pastorally and nostalgically. With "*Spasmodic party music*" (281) the partiers get caught up in cheerfull small talk. Liz praises this civil party, deeply impressed.

> I think this is such a gorgeous party. . . . I think it's such fun. . . . Oh God I don't know, elegance, style, grace, taste, don't these words, these concepts, mean anything any more? I'm not alone, am I, in thinking them incredibly important? (299)

Though civility seems to cover the stage, the shadow of fear is caught in Dusty's repeated questions about the whereabouts of his brother Jimmy who hasn't come to the party yet: "Does anyone know what's happened to my brother Jimmy?" (296). Melissa, who came late, says,

> The town's dead. There's nobody on the street, there's not a soul in sight, apart from some . . . soldiers. My driver had to stop at a . . . you know . . . what do you call it? . . . a roadblock. (286)

As if to respond to her question, when Fred asks Douglas, "How's it going tonight?" Douglas says, "Like clockwork . . . we want peace and we're going to get it" (292). Their conversation suggests that some military action is occurring in the streets during the party, and Gavin admits the "round-up" in his closing speech of the party, saying "we've had a bit of a round-up this evening. This round-up is coming to an end" (313). From their words, we can suspect that Gavin, Fred and Douglas are personally related to state power. There are no direct words from them in the drama which identify them as power's agents. But when we hear the host of this party Gavin say,

> In fact normal services will be resumed shortly. . . . That's all we ask, that the service this country provides will run on normal, secure and legitimate paths and that the ordinary citizen be allowed to pursue his labours and his leisure in peace. (313)

we are reminded of the nearness of civility and barbarity in power. A peaceful party host Gavin seems to disguise himself as an ordinary citizen here. Charles Grimes argues that "Politesse, culture, distinction, refinement . . . and other practices of 'everyday life' disguise an ugly, otherwise naked will to power . . ." (103). That power's barbarity lurks invisibly in civility is expressed in "elegance," "grace," which Liz mentions about the partygoers' dresses, and the "normal services" which Gavin assures will resume.

And at the end we encounter the victim Jimmy who appears from offstage: "Martin Regal . . . sees Jimmy as dead at this moment" (Grime 125). He *"comes out of the light and stands in the doorway,"* on the stage while *"Everyone is still, in silhouette"* (313). The paradoxical contrast of light to both sides illuminates the cruelty hidden in civility. Jimmy says enigmatically before the curtain falls:

> ... a door bangs, I hear voices, then it stops. Everything stops. ... It shuts. It all shuts. ... I see nothing at any time any more. I sit sucking the dark. ... The dark is in my mouth and I suck it. It's the only thing I have. ... I suck it. (314)

From his words we realize that he was arrested in the round-up, put in prison and killed, which the repeated words "the dark" imply strongly. "The dark" he sucks recalls the Enlightenment whose aim was to 'enlighten' people. As seen above, the new power born in the period is a disciplinary one whose "chief function" is "to 'train'" (Foucault 170). And it is "exercised through its invisibility" (187). As "the progressive aspect of the Enlightenment finally betrayed itself with the technology of atrocity" (Knowles 59) in the twentieth century, a barbarous aspect was latent invisibly in power in the Enlightenment.

Power's opposite phases does the play, at the end of it, reveal by inserting the fantastic appearance of the dead Jimmy into a realistic rendering of the party, like the Brechtian effect of alienation. Pinter exposes civil power's latent cruelty in this play with such modernist double awareness. On that point, power's barbarity is finally somewhat visible on the stage. But is there anyone in this play who impresses nakedly the supreme authority of power like Nicolas in *One for the Road*? Gavin? No. He is only "connected to the authoritarian apparatus" (Baker-White 66). Seen from the view that his relation to power is described vaguely and obliquely, he has no intention of disguising power's authority. On the contrary, power is diffused into some subjects rather than concentrated in one person. None of the characters is an autonomous subject who exercises state power. Silverstein argues,

> Pinter ... conceptualizes the subject's relation to power in more Foucaultian terms: the subject remains an *effect* that emerges from the operations of a Power that remains irreducible to the dimensions of that subject. (*"One"* 438)

According to Silverstein, in Pinter "the subject of (and to) power is 'expendable'" because power "can produce other candidates to fill its subject positions" (*"One"* 439). If so, Gavin as well as Fred and Douglas is no more than power's instrument. Fred implies hesitatingly in his dialogues with Charlotte that he is an exchangeable tool of power:

> CHARLOTTE. I think there's something going on in the street.
> FRED. Leave the street to us.
> CHARLOTTE. Who's us?
> FRED. Oh, just us ... you know.   (307)

His ambiguous and vague reply implies that he is one of "us" or power's instruments.

The problem of the self or subject in the play is condensed into a question by power's victim, Jimmy: "What am I?" (314). He says in his monologue "I had a name. It was Jimmy," and then "When everything is quiet I hear my heart" (313). His meaning here is that his identity was Jimmy in quiet and peaceful days. He continues,

> When the terrible noises come I don't hear anything. Don't hear don't breathe am blind.
>
> Then everything is quiet. I hear a heartbeat. It is probably not my

7   *One for the Road, Party Time, Celebration* and Power's Invisibility

>   heartbeat. It is probably someone else's heartbeat. (314)

What he tries to convey here is that Jimmy was killed in power's round-up ("the terrible noises"), and he has changed into another victim (he hears "someone else's heartbeat"). In other words, it indicates that power's victims are also exchangeable. Jimmy becomes representative of victims in general at the end. Thus as he has lost the self or the subject, he is asking who he is.

All of the characters in the play have neither self nor the subjectivity. This is impressed strongly by the way people's conversations are scattered incoherently in the shadow of the round-up offstage. The world of this play is, as it were, a postmodern one. Though Grimes argues that power in the play is "Western capitalist power" (102) and that of "the fascist regime" (103), power here seems to be a more modern power in "the global system of consumer capitalism" (Robert Gordon 190) in which the subject is fictitious and fragmented.

4

R. Gordon recognizes the power in global consumer capitalism more conspicuously in *Celebration*. This play, unlike *Party Time*, unrolls only the phases of civility and doesn't present even a recognizably suggestive hint of invisible barbarism, both onstage and offstage. The stage shows us a stylish restaurant in which two middle-aged bourgeois couples are celebrating the wedding anniversary of Lambert and Julie, and at the other table a young banker Russell and his wife Suki are dining. Though the play unfolds incoherently at the two tables with wandering conversations of civility, like those at the cocktail party in *Party Time*, their talk is more vulgar and represented more satirically. The level of their sophistication is manifested symbolically to the point that they don't know what they have seen before dinner, a play or a ballet or an opera.

> RICHARD. Very very well, been to a play?
> MATT. No. The ballet. (455)

> SONIA. Been to the theatre?
> SUKI. The opera. (463)

Moreover Lambert, a rich snob, is ignorant of what kind of dish Osso Bucco is despite his own ordering: "Osso what?" (440). Osso Bucco is to him only a sexual reminder of "arsehole."

> LAMBERT. Well I knew Osso was Italian but I know bugger all about Bucco.
> MATT. I didn't know arsehole was Italian. (441)

Their conversations are full of gibes, piss-taking, sexual affairs, and monetary concerns. Russell calls his wife Suki "a whore" (449) while Prue piss-takes Richard, the maitre d', saying "she [Julie] could make a better sauce than yours if she pissed into it" (458). When they find out that Lambert at table one and Suki at table two were acquaintances before, Russell replies that they met and had sex "Behind a filing cabinet" to Prue's question "I wonder where these two met" (493). Lambert is proud of his wealth ("Do you know how much money I made last year?" [451]), and shows how nouveau riche he is by giving a few fifty-pound notes as a tip to Sonia, Richard's assistant, saying indecently "Stick them in your suspenders" (503). The servile Richard and Sonia try to ingratiate themselves with their best customers. When Lambert makes fun of Richard, saying, "You could tickle his arse with a feather," Richard replies fawningly, "Well, I'm so glad. . . ." (459) while Sonia *"giggles"* longingly to Lambert's dangling *"the notes in front of her cleavage"* (503). About these gross situations and the materialism of the guests in the restaurant, Gordon says,

> The play exposes the way postmodern culture not only fragments but flattens hierarchies of value so that the difference between one pleasure and another is merely a matter of price. (191)

It is certainly true that in this play civility is depicted from the viewpoint of the postmodern situation where "the postmodern body . . . is now exposed to a perceptual barrage of immediacy from which all sheltering layers and intervening mediations have been removed" (Jameson 412-13). As R. Gordon says, the restaurant is "a kind of temple" whose function is "appeasing its diners by offering them sensory pleasures and the comfort of exclusive privilege as gratification designed to dull their naked fear and aggression" (191).

Thus civility seems to cover all the play even if its vulgarity is satirized. But the barbarism of power is hidden behind civility in this play, too. R. Gordon agrees:

> Beneath the stylish surface of the restaurant, the world these characters actually inhabit operates according to the principle of repression by brute force. (191)

But unlike the round-up offstage in *Party Time*, no evidence of the barbarity of power is perceived, even offstage. Power is completely invisible in *Celebration*. Power's disguise is implied indirectly, metaphorically and analogically.

the telescopic lens.

....

My grandfather introduced me the mystery of life and I'm still in the middle of it. I can't find the door to get out. My grandfather got out of it. He got right out of it. He left it behind him and he didn't look back.

....

And I'd like to make one further interjection.
He stands still.
Slow fade. (508)

In the first four lines, the Waiter shows the world of new modernity, Heisenberg's 'Uncertainty principle,' through the image of the "telescope" which becomes a symbol of the world's indeterminacy, not absoluteness, from its image of enlarging the world. The world of the three a's began from such new view of science in the early twentieth century. People who live in such a world have lost the meaning of life and feel alone or alienated, losing the absolute. The Waiter's grandfather "knew these people where they were isolated, where they were alone," and tried to help them like "Christ" (502).

The Waiter is one of them, too. He has got lost in "the mystery of life," and cannot "find the door to get out," so that he is wounded. To such a man, the diners, who are the tools of power, seem to threaten obliquely to have him sacked, pretending to favor him.

RUSSELL. You going to stay until it changes hands?
WAITER. Are you suggesting that I'm about to get the boot?
SUKI. They wouldn't do that to a nice lad like you. (468)

Grimes says about the situation of the Waiter that "he is . . . sharply excluded from the world controlled by the diners" (131), and that "his final silence poignantly illustrates his ultimate dispossession" (132). Although Lambert gives a fifty-pound note as a tip to him, this ostensible civility of kindness hides barbarity. Begley argues that "The brutality of this [postmodern] culture lies less in what it depicts than in what it conceals" (185).

Pinter shows double awareness in this play, too, which R. Gordon calls a "blend of realism and abstraction" (*Harold* 193). He depicts both the people in the restaurant and the way civility pervades the play in the mode of realism, but by interjecting the Waiter's implausible and fantastic remembrance of his grandfather, he makes the realistic rendering of civility fictitious or suspicious in the manner of Brecht's effect of alienation, and betrays the barbarity hidden in civility and the void beneath a joyfully noisy postmodern culture, showing the individual or self as a schizoid subject and a disposable tool of power.

The Waiter plays the role of victim of such culture and power at the same time as he assumes that of the whistle-blower of the status quo. Thus he, as an absurdist, like the modernist writers referred to in his monologues, feels "the mystery of life" in the void, alienated and excluded from the shallow world of consumer culture with power invisible. We can see the absurdist Pinter reflected in the Waiter.

It is well known that Pinter was influenced by absurdist writers Beckett and Kafka, whose names are in the Waiter's interjections. He is, "like these two writers, preoccupied with man at the limit of his being" (Esslin, *Theatre* 261). According to Esslin, Pinter said that "he was dealing with his characters 'at the extreme edge of their living, where they are living pretty much alone'" (*Theatre* 262). While Pinter reflects an absurdist phase in this lost Waiter, he mirrors another of his phases, as a political activist in his later years, in the Waiter as an indirect critic of the status quo.

In 1987 Pinter participated in a protest at the American Embassy on the reason that under the pretext of the protection of democracy the US militarily and financially supported Contra terrorist groups, who attempted to overthrow the Sandinista government in Nicaragua. In 1998 he wrote a letter to the Prime Minister Tony Blair in which he said, "It [the US] has given and still gives total support to the Turkish government's campaign of genocide against the Kurdish people" ("Open Letter" 256). In a string of these protest activities Pinter expressed his "outrage at the hypocrisy of Western governments—claiming moral superiority, while sanctioning the most extreme cruelties . . ." (Billington 305). By his political actions, he questions civil democratic regimes' hiding of barbarity.

> . . . it's not simply that the United States, in my view, has created the most appalling state of affairs all over the world for many years, it's also that what we call our democracies have subscribed to these repressive, cynical and indifferent acts of murder. We sell arms to all the relevant countries, do we not? Not just the United States, but also Great Britain, France, Germany *and* Spain are very active in this field. And they still pat themselves on the back and call themselves a democracy. ("Writing, Politics" 247)

Thus Pinter, in his last full-length play, depicts power's disguise in a contemporary postmodern society under consumer capitalism, like "post-Thatcherite Britain, a society dominated by greed and dumbed-down educational and intellectual standards" (Esslin, "Harold Pinter" 29), in which the self or the subject, fragmented, decentered and schizophrenic, is a tool of power while power permeates civility in everyday life and democracy invisibly with its barbarity hidden. Pinter was irritated at such an irresponsible and deceitful society in his later life.

> Mrs Thatcher, I remind you, said immortally: 'There is no such thing as society.' . . . She meant by it that we have no obligation or responsibility to anyone else other than ourselves. This has encouraged the most appalling greed and corruption in my society.
> ("Writing, Politics" 250)

> . . . the majority of politicians . . . are interested not in truth but in power and in the maintenance of that power. To maintain that power it is essential that people remain in ignorance, that they live in ignorance of the truth, even the truth of their own lives. What surrounds us therefore is a vast tapestry of lies, upon which we feed.
> ("Art, Truth" 288)

The later three plays reflect Pinter's views of the self, the world and power in his later years very ingeniously but insistently. The epitome is represented metaphorically very well in the Waiter's third speech in *Celebration*, as Grimes says, "Pinter is playing a double game in this passage, equating torture victims with cultural icons. . . . he also imagistically merges the suffering, marginalized artist with the suffering, marginalized victim of political violence" (133).

Notes
1. On Henry V's disguise and Duke Vincentio's one in *Measure for Measure*, see Hosokawa 155-77, 229-59.
2. On Prospero's disguise, see Hosokawa 387-409.

Works Cited

Adler, Thomas P. "From Flux to Fixity: Art and Death in Pinter's *No Man's Land*." *Critical Essays on Harold Pinter*. Ed. Steven H. Gale. Boston: G. K. Hall & Co, 1990. 136-41.

Angel-Perez, Elizabeth. "*Ashes to Ashes*, Pinter's Dibbuks." *Viva Pinter: Harold Pinter's Spirit of Resistance*. Ed. Brigitte Gauthier. Bern: Peter Lang, 2009. 139-60.

Aragay, Mireia. "Pinter, Politics and Postmodernism (2)." *The Cambridge Companion to Harold Pinter*. Ed. Peter Raby. Cambridge: Cambridge University Press, 2001. 246-59.

Baker-White, Robert. "Violence and Festivity in Harold Pinter's *The Birthday Party, One for the Road, and Party Time*." *The Pinter Review: Annual Essays 1994 (1995)*: 61-75.

Baumer, Franklin L. *Modern European Thought: Continuity and Change in Ideas, 1600-1950*. New York: Macmillan Publishing, 1977.

Begley, Varum. *Harold Pinter and the Twilight of Modernism*. Toronto: University of Toronto Press, 2005.

Behera, Guru Charan. *Reality and Illusion in the Plays of Harold Pinter*. New Delhi: Atlantic Publishers and Distributors, 1998.

Bell, Michael. "The Metaphysics of Modernism." *The Cambridge Companion to Modernism*. Ed. Michael Levenson. Cambridge: Cambridge University Press, 1999. 9-32.

Belsey, Catherine. *The Subject of Tragedy: Identity and Difference in Renaissance Drama*. London. Routledge and Kegan Paul, 1977.

Berry, Edward. *Shakespeare's Comic Rites*. Cambridge: Cambridge University Press, 1984.

Billington, Michael. *Harold Pinter*. 1996. London: Faber and Faber, 2007.

Bradbrook, M. C. *The Growth and Structure of Elizabethan Comedy*. 1955. Cambridge: Cambridge University Press, 1973.

____. "Shakespeare and the Use of Disguise in Elizabethan Drama." *Essays in Criticism* 2 (1952): 159-68.

Bradbury, Malcolm, and James McFarlane. "The Name and Nature of Modernism." *Modernism: A Guide to European Literature 1890-1930*. Ed. Malcolm Bradbury and James McFarlane. 1976. London: Penguin Books, 1991. 19-55.

Brown, John Russell."Mr. Pinter's Shakespeare." *The Critical Quarterly* 5 (1963): 251-65.

Burkman, Katherine H. "Death and the Double in Three Plays by Harold Pinter." *Harold Pinter: You Never Heard Such Silence*. Ed. Alan Bold. London : Vision Press. 1985. 131-45.

____. "Harold Pinter's *Ashes to Ashes*: Rebecca and Devil as Albert Speer." *The Pinter Review: Collected Essays 1997 and 1998* (1998): 86-96.

Cahn, Victor L. *Gender and Power in the Plays of Harold Pinter*. London: Macmillan, 1994.

Carpenter, Charles A. "'What Have I seen, The Scum or the Essence?': Symbolic Fallout in Pinter's *Birthday Party*." *Modern Drama* 17 (1974): 389-402.

Cartwright, Kent. *Theatre and Humanism: English Drama in the Sixteenth Century*. Cambridge: Cambridge University Press, 1999.

Davis, Lloyd. *Guise and Disguise: Rhetoric and Characterization in the English Renaissance*. Toronto: University of Toronto Press, 1975.

Diamond, Elin. *Pinter's Comic Play*. London: Associated University Press, 1985.

Dobrez, L. A. C. *The Existential and Its Exits: Literary and Philosophical Perspectives on the Works of Beckett, Ionesco, Genet & Pinter*. London:

Athlone Press, 1986.

Dollimore, Jonathan. *Radical Tragedy: Religion, Ideology and Power in the Drama of Shakespeare and His Contemporaries*. 1984. Brighton: The Harvester Press, 1986.

Dukore, Bernand F. "A Woman's Place." *The Quarterly Journal o Speech* 52 (1966): 237-41.

____. "The Theatre of Harold Pinter." *The Tulane Drama Review* 6 (1962): 43-54.

Eagleton, Terry. *The Illusions of Postmodernism*. Oxford: Blackwell, 1996.

Esslin, Martin. "Harold Pinter: from *Moonlight* to *Celebration*." *The Pinter Review : Annual Essays 1999-2000* (2001): 23-30.

____. "Harold Pinter's Theatre of Cruelty." *Pinter at Sixty*. Ed. Katherine H . Burkman and John L. Kundert-Gibbs. Bloomington: Indiana University Press, 1993. 27-36.

____. "Modernist Drama: Dedekind to Brecht." *Modernism: A Guide to European Literature 1890-1930*. Ed. Malcolm Bradbury and James McFarlane. 1976. London. Penguin Books. 1991. 527-60.

____. *The Peopled Wound: The Work of Harold Pinter*. New York: Doubleday, 1970.

____. *Pinter: The Playwright*. 1970. London: Methuen, 1992.

____. *The Theatre of the Absurd*. 1961. New York: Vintage Books, 2001.

Foucault, Michel. *Discipline and Punish: The Birth of the Prison*. Trans. Alan Sheridan. 1975. New York: Vintage Books, 1979.

Gale, Steven H. *Butter's Going Up: A Critical Analysis of Harold Pinter's Work*. Durham: Duke University Press, 1977.

Ganz, Arthur. "A Clue to the Pinter Puzzle: The Triple Self in *"The Homecoming."* *Educational Theatre Journal* 21 (1969): 180-87.

Giamatti, A. Bartlett. *Exile and Change in Renaissance Literature*. New Haven: Yale University Press, 1984.

Gillen, Francis. "History as a Single Act: Pinter's *Ashes to Ashes.*" *Cycnos* 14 (1997) : 91-97.

Gordon, Lois G. *Stratagems to Uncover Nakedness: The Dramas of Harold Pinter*. Columbia: University of Missouri Press, 1969.

Gordon, Robert. *Harold Pinter: The Theatre of Power*. Ann Arbor: University of Michigan Press, 2012.

Grimes, Charles. *Harold Pinter's Politics: A Silence beyond Echo*. Rutherford, NL: Fairleigh Dickinson University Press. 2005.

Gussow, Mel. *Conversations with Pinter*. New York: Grove Press, 1994.

Herf, Jeffrey. *Reactionary Modernism: Technology, Culture, and Politics in Weimar and the Third Reich*. Cambridge: Cambridge University Press, 1984.

Horkheimer, Max, and Theodor W. Adorno. *Dialect of Enlightenment*. Trans. John Cumming. 1944. New York: Continuum, 1997.

Hosokawa, Makoto. *Kyo to Jitu no Hazama de: Shakespeare no Disguise no Keifu (Between Essence and Construct: The Genealogy of Disguise in Shakespeare)*. Tokyo: Eihosha. 2003.

Innes, Christopher. "Modernism in Drama." *The Cambridge Companion to Modernism*. Ed.Michael Levenson. Cambridge: Cambridge University Press, 1999. 130--56.

Irigaray, Luce. *This Sex Which Is Not One*. Trans. Catherine Porter with Caroline Burke. Ithaca NY: Cornell University Press, 1985.

Jameson, Fredric. *Postmodernism, or, the Cultural Logic of Late Capitalism*. Durham: Duke University Press, 1991.

Jiji, Vera M. "Pinter's Four Dimensional House: *The Homecoming.*" *Critical Essays on Harold Pinter*. Ed. Steven H. Gale. Boston: G. K. Hall, 1990. 101-10.

Kahn, Coppélia. *Man's Estate: Masculine Identity in Shakespeare*. Berkeley: University of California Press, 1981.

Knowles, Ronald. *Understanding Harold Pinter*. Columbia: University of South Carolina Press, 1995.

Kott, Jan. *Shakespeare Our Contemporary*. London: Methuen, 1965.

Laity, Susan. "The Soul of Man under Victoria: *Iolanthe, The Importance of Being Earnest*, and Bourgeois Drama." *Modern Critical Interpretations: Oscar Wilde's The Importance of Being Earnest*. Ed. Harold Bloom. New York: Chelsea House, 1988. 119-46.

Lindner, Robert, and M. Rebel. *Without a Cause: The Story of a Criminal Psychopath*. 1971. New York: Other Press, 2003.

Littleton, Betty J., ed. *Clyomon and Clamydes*. The Hague: Mouton, 1968.

Lunn, Eugene. *Marxism and Modernism: An Historical Study of Lukacs, Brecht, Benjamine and Adorno*. 1982. Berkeley: University of California Press, 1984.

Machiavelli, Niccolò. *The Prince*. Ed. & Trans. Robert M. Adams. 1977. New York: W. W. Norton, 1992.

Pico della Mirandola, Giovanni. *Oration on the Dignity of Man. The Renaissance Philosophy of Man*. Ed. Ernst Cassier, Paul Oskar Kristeller, John Herman Randall, Jr. 1948. Chicago: Chicago University Press, 1956. 223-54.

Pinter, Harold. *Ashes to Ashes*. London: Fabor and Fabor, 1996.

____. "Art, Truth and Politics: The Nobel Lecture." *Harold Pinter Various Voices: Sixty Years of Prose, Poetry, Politics 1948-2008*. 1998. London: Faber and Faber, 2009. 285-300.

____. *The Birthday Party*. 1st ed. London: Encore Publishing, 1959.

____. *The Birthday Party*. Rev. ed. *Plays: One*. London: Methuen. 1989.

____. *The Caretaker. Plays*: *Two*. London: Methuen, 1988.

____. *Celebration. Harold Pinter:Plays Four*. London: Faber and Faber, 2005.

____. *Collected Poems and Prose*. New York: Grove Press, 1996.

____. *The Collection. Plays:Two*. London: Methuen, 1988.

____. *The Dumb Waiter*. *Plays: One*. London: Methuen. 1989.

____. "Harold Pinter and Michael Billington in Conversation at the National Theatre, 26 October 1996." *Harold Pinter Various Voices:Sixty Years of Prose, Poetry, Politics 1948-2008*. London: Faber and Faber, 2009.74-83.

____. *The Homecoming*. *Plays:Three*. London: Methuen, 1989.

____. *The Lover*. *Plays:Two*. London: Methuen, 1988.

____. *Mountain Language*. *Harold Pinter: Plays Four*. London: Faber and Faber, 2005.

____. *No Man's Land*. *Plays:Four*. London: Methuen, 1986.

____. *Old Times*. *Plays: Four*. London: Methuen, 1986.

____. *One for the Road*. *Harold Pinter: Plays Four*. London: Faber and Faber, 2005.

____. "An Open Letter to the Prime Minister: *Guardian*, 17 February 1998." *Harold Pinter Various Voices: Sixty Years of Prose, Poetry, Politics 1948-2008*. 1998. London: Faber and Faber, 2009. 255-57.

____. *Party Time*. *Harold Pinter: Plays Four*. London: Faber and Faber, 2005.

____. "A Speech of Thanks." *Harold Pinter Various Voices: Sixty Years of Prose, Poetry, Politics* 1948-2008 . 1998. London; Faber and Faber, 2009. 69-73.

____. "Writing for Myself." Introduction. *Plays: Two*. London: Methuen, 1988. 9-12.

____. "Writing for the Theatre." Introduction. *Plays: One*. London: Methuen, 1989. 9-16.

____. "Writing, Politics and *Ashes to Ashes*." *Harold Pinter Various Voices: Sixty Years of Prose, Poetry, Politics 1948-2008*. 1998. London: Faber and Faber, 2009. 238-54.

Prinz, Jessica. "'You Brought It upon Yourself': Subjectivity and Culpability in *Ashes to Ashes*." *The Pinter Review: Collected Essays 2001 and 2002* (2002): 97-105.

Quigley, Austin E. "Design and Discovery in Pinter's *The Lover.*" *Harold Pinter:Critical Approaches*. Ed.Steven H. Gale. London and Toronto: Associated University Presses,1986. 82-101.

Redford, John. *Wit and Science. Medieval Drama*. Ed. David Bevington. Boston: Houghton Mifflin Company, 1975. 1029-61.

Sakellaridou, Elizabeth. *Pinter's Portraits: A Study of Female Characters in the Plays of Harold Pinter*. Totowa: Barnes & Noble Books, 1988.

Sereny, Gitta. *Albert Speer: His Battle with Truth*. 1995. London: Picador, 1996.

Shakespeare, William. *As You Like It*. Ed. Agnes Latham. London: Methuen, 1975.

———. *The Comedy of Errors*. Ed. R. A. Foakes. London: Methuen, 1962.

———. *Hamlet*. Ed. Harold Jenkins. London: Mdthuen, 1982.

———. *Macbeth*. Ed. A. R. Braunmuller. Cambridge: Cambridge University Press, 1997.

———. *TheMerchant of Venice*. Ed. John Russell Brown. London: Methuen, 1955.

———. *A Midsummer Night's Dream*. Ed. Harold F. Brooks. London: Methuen, 1979.

———. *Othello*. Ed. M. R. Ridley. London: Methuen, 1969.

———. *The Taming of the Shrew*. Ed. Brian Morris. London: Methuen, 1981.

———. *The Tempest*. Ed. Frank Kermode. London: Methuen, 1969.

———.*The Tragedy of King Lear*. Ed. Jay L. Halio. Cambridge: Cambridge University Press, 1992.

Silverstein, Marc. *Harold Pinter and the Language of Cultural Power*. Lewisburg: Bucknell University Press, 1993.

———. "*One for the Road, Mountain Language* and the Impasse of Politics." *Modern Drama* 34 (1991): 422-40.

———. "'Talking about Some Kind of Atrocity': *Ashes to Ashes* in Barcelona."

The Pinter Review: Collected Essays 1997 and 1998 (1999): 74-85.

Suter, Anthony. "The Dual Character and the Image of the Artist in Pinter's *'No Man's Land.'" Durham University Journal* 75 (1984): 89-94.

Taylor, Charles. *Sources of the Self: The Making of the Modern Identity.* Cambridge: Harvard University Press, 1989.

Taylor, John Russell. *Anger and After: A Guide to the New British Drama.* 1962. London: Eyre Methuen, 1977.

Thompson, David T. *Pinter: The Player's Playwright.* London: Macmillan, 1985.

Udal, Nicholas. *Respublica.* Ed. W. W. Creg. London: Oxford University Press, 1952.

Wellwarth, George E. "*The Dumb Waiter, The Collection, The Lover,* and *The Homecoming*: A Revisionist Approach." *Pinter at 70.* Ed. Lois Gordon. London: Routledge, 2001. 95-108.

Wilde, Oscar. *The Decay of Lying. The Complete Works of Oscar Wilde.* Ed. J. B. Foreman. Vyvyan Holland. New York: Harper Perennial, 1989. 970-92.

____. *The Importance of Being Earnest. The Complete Works of Oscar Wilde.* Ed. J. B.Foreman. Vyvyan Holland. New York: Harper Perennial, 1989. 321-84.

____. *The Soul of Man under Socialism. The Complete Works of Oscar Wilde.* Ed. J. B. Foreman. Vyvyan Holland. New York: Harper Perennial, 1989. 1079-104

Wind, Edgar. *Pagan Mysteries in the Renaissance.* London: Faber and Faber, 1958.

Wixson, Christopher. "'I'm Compelled to Ask You Questions': Interrogative Comedy and Harold Pinter's *Ashes to Ashes.*" *The Pinter Review: Collected Essays 2003 and 2004* (2004): 7-28.

Wycherley, William. *The Country Wife.* Ed. James Ogden. 1973. London: A&C Black, 2003.

Index

[A]

Adler, Thomas P., 96
Adorno, Theodor W., and Max Horkheimer: *Dialect of Enlightenment*, 106, 111
androgyny, 58
Angel-Perez, Elizabeth, 103, 104, 107
Aragay, Mireia, 114, 123
Arden, John, 36
"Art, Truth and Politics: TheNobel Lecture", 29, 30, 142
Ashes to Ashes, 103-19
As You Like It, 5, 10, 29, 58, 66, 78
Auschwitz, 35, 111, 137

[B]

Baker-White, Robert, 130
barbarism, 35, 121, 132, 134, 136, 137, 140
Basement, The, 79
Baumer, L. Franklin, 2, 3, 6, 22, 35, 37, 43, 48, 90, 112
Beckett, Samuel, 48, 140
becoming, 3, 92
Begley, Varun, 2, 24, 36, 39-41, 46, 121, 123, 125
Behera, Guru Charan, 22, 56, 81
being, 2
Bell, Michael, 3, 4, 44, 67, 68, 85
Belsey, Catherine, 9, 43, 48
Bentham, Jeremy, the Panopticon, 126, 138
Bergson, Henri, 92
Berry, Edward, 66, 97, 101
Betrayal, 67, 107
Birthday Party, The, 2, 9-31, 36, 75
Billington, Michael, 7, 106, 118, 141

Blair, Tony, 141
Bradbrook, M. C., 5, 13, 33, 42, 43, 49, 58, 104, 124
Bosnia, 107
Bradbury, Malcolm and James McFarlane, 3, 20, 92
Brathwait, Richard:*The English Gentleman*, 48
Brechtian effect of alienation, 22, 130, 140
Brown, John Russell, 6
Buchenwald, 107
Burkman, Katherine H., 90, 101, 116

[C]

Cahn, Victor L., 76
capitalism, advanced, 20, 27, 28; consumer, 132, 141; late, 27, 138
Caretaker, The, 3, 6, 33-49, 74, 88
Carpenter, Charles A., 17, 20
Cartwright, Kent, 70, 84, 104, 105, 116, 117, 118
Celebration, 121-22, 132-42
chain of being, 3, 43, 58
Clyomon and Clamydes, 118
Collected Poems and Prose, 31
Collection, The, 1, 6, 51-58, 69
Comedy of Errors, The, 49, 58, 66, 97, 101
Country Wife, The, 44, 45
Cymbelline, 48

[D]

Davis, Lloyd, 5, 23, 48, 125
Descartes, René, 4
Diamond, Elin, 12, 72, 94
discordia concors, 42
disguise, 3, 7, 29, 38, 39, 41, 43, 124,

151

125; in *Ashes to Ashes*, 103-05, 114-15; in *The Birthday Party*, 10, 12-13, 16, 18, 23-24, 40; in *The Caretaker*, 33, 37-38, 45, 47-48; in *The Celebration*, 121; in *The Homecoming*, 83-84; in *The Lover*, 58-62; in *One for the Road*, 124-25; in *Party Time*, 129; in Shakespeare, 5, 13, 16, 43, 48, 58, 66, 78, 83-84, 104, 122, 124, 125, 127, 142; in Wilde (*The Importance of Being Earnest*), 41-42; in Wycherley (*The Country Wife*), 44, 45

Dobrez, L.A.C., 67, 68, 74, 76, 80, 85, 87, 98

Dollimore, Jonathan, 11, 43

doppelgänger, 25, 87

Dora, 108

double, in *The Birthday Party*, 24, 26, 28; in *No Man's Land*, 90-91, 94, 97, 99; in Shakespeare (*The Comedy of Errors*), 49, 58, 66

double awareness, 'Ancient', 3, 4, 78; modern, 1, 2, 4, 6, 9, 21, 51-52, 64, 97, 117, 124;

Dukore, Bernard F., 9, 30, 68

Dumb Waiter, The, 6, 22, 29, 31, 69

Dwarfs, The, 27, 75

[E]

Eagleton, Terry, 4, 29, 35, 85, 113, 114, 136

Eddington, Arthur, 4

Eliot, T. S.: *The Four Quartets*, 87

Enlightenment, the, 35, 43, 111, 130, 137

Ephesians, 16

Esslin, Martin, 9, 12, 24, 29, 46, 53, 58, 73, 76, 86, 87, 101, 111, 140, 141

expressionism, 85, 89, 90

expressionist drama, 25, 87

Everyman, 12

[F]

fascism, 106, 109

Foucault, Michel, 126, 130

[G]

Gale, Steven H., 9, 11, 15, 18, 88

Gammer Gurton's Needle, 13

Ganz, Arthur, 73, 77

Genesis, 6

Giamatti, A. Bartlett, 6

Gillen, Francis, 107, 115, 117, 118

Gordon, Lois G., 9, 24, 38

Gordon, Robert, 18, 23, 132, 134, 140

Grimes, Charles, 18, 129, 132, 136, 140, 142

Gussow, Mel, 20, 92, 94

[H]

Hackney Down, 7, 118

Halio, Jay L., 101

Hamlet, 12, 29, 104

Hegel, G. W. F., 35

Heidegger, Martin, 28, 92, 112

Heisenberg's 'Uncertainty principle', 2, 3, 5, 20, 139

Henry V, 122, 142

Herf, Jeffrey, 35, 111, 118

Hitler, Adolf, 18, 106

Holbein: *The Ambassadors*, 67

Homecoming, The, 29, 67-86, 105

Holocaust, 103, 105, 107, 116

Hosokawa, Makoto, 48, 86, 142

humanist drama, 5, 104, 116

Hume, David, 85

Husserl, Edmund, 28

hypothetical future, 97, 101

[I]

Ibsen, Henrik, 67

idealism, 5

Importance of Being Earnest, The, 38, 41-42, 44-45

Innes, Christopher, 87
improvisation, 38, 90, 92, 98, 112
Ionesco, Eugène, 98
Irigaray, Luce, 83
Irish Republican Army (IRA), 23
[J]
Jameson, Fredric, 36, 134, 138
Jiji, Vera M., 73, 76
Joyce, James, 2
[K]
Kafka, Franz, 140
Kahn, Coppélia, 84
Kant, Immanuel, 35, 43
King David, 30
King Lear, 29, 92
Knowles, Ronald, 21, 23, 24, 117
Kott, Jan, 92
[L]
Lacan, Jacques, 30; mirror stage, 22
Laity, Susan, 45
liberal (essentialist) humanism, 11, 35, 43, 113
Lindner, Robert M., 136
'low intensity conflict', 30
Lover, The, 1, 58-65, 69
Lunn, Eugene, 65, 106, 137
[M]
Macbeth, 27, 115, 118
Machiavelli, Niccolò: *The Prince*, 122; and disguise, 124, 125
Man, Thomas, 2
Mankind, 70
Marlowe, Christopher, 4
McMaster, Anew, 10, 78, 86, 118
Measure for Measure, 122, 127, 142
Medwall: *Nature*, 13, 70
memory plays, 87, 96
Merchant of Venice, The, 6, 29, 42, 58, 78
Midsummer Night's Dream, A, 96

mimicry, 83
misogyny, 70
Miss Julie, 67
modernism, 2, 3, 6, 20, 24, 27, 36, 37, 137, 138
modernist negation, 36, 46, 47
modernity, new, 2, 3, 6, 37, 43, 44, 90-91, 92, 112, 137; old, 2, 43, 45, 110, 112, 137
morality plays, 13
Mountain Language, 127
Murdoch, Iris, 4
[N]
Natham, the prophet, 30
Nazism, 18, 105, 107, 108, 111, 114, 117, 118, 121
naturalism, 3, 67
neo-platonism, 4
Newton, Sir Isaac, 3; and mechanistic world view, 2, 3, 4, 35, 44, 51, 58
nihilism, 90, 100, 112
Nobel lecture ("Art, Truth, and Politics"), 29, 30
No Man's Land, 87-101, 105
[O]
Old Times, 87, 107
One for the Road, 121-27, 136
"Open Letter to the Prime Minister, An" 141
Ortega y Gasset, 90, 100
Other, he, 7, 9, 22, 26
Othello, 5, 10, 12, 13, 29
[P]
Party Time, 121-22, 128-32
Pico della Mirandola, Giovanni: *Oration on the Dignity of Man*, 4, 5, 42, 84
Pinter, Harold, 1, 2, 5, 29, 33, 53, 58, 78, 94, 103; as absurd dramatist, 6, 87, 140; as activist, 20, 30, 118-19, 141-42;

153

as Shakespearian player, 5, 78, 86, 117
postmodernism, 113, 117, 132, 134, 136, 140
post-realism, 7
power, capitalist, 132; disciplinary, 126, 127; on display, 126
Prinz, Jessica, 103, 107, 112, 116
Promethean man, 34, 35
Protean man, 4, 42
psychological realism, 67
psychopath, 135-36
[Q]
Quigley, Austin W., 66
[R]
Raphael: *Dream of Scipio*, 75; *The Three Graces*, 75, 77
Realism, 1, 2, 3, 4, 7, 10, 18-19, 20, 21, 22, 40-41, 46, 51, 55, 67-71, 73, 76, 77, 82, 85, 87, 88, 93, 97, 99, 107, 110, 140
realist mimesis, 4
Redford, John: *Wit and Science*, 104-105
Resnais, Alain: *Night and Fog*, 121
Rousseau, Jean-Jacques, 35
[S]
Sakellaridou, Elizabeth, 63, 77
Sade, Marquis de, 111, 118
schizophrenia, 27, 28
self (subject), 6, 15, 39, 42, 43, 47, 48, 51, 65, 75, 85, 113, 114, 122, 136, 138; in *Ashes to Ashes*, 105, 110, 110-14, 116; in *The Birthday Party*; 9-15, 18-20, 22-29; in *The Caretaker*, 33, 37-48; in *Celebration*, 141, 142; in *The Collection*, 53-60; in *The Homecoming*, 67, 68, 72-76, 79-80, 84-85; in *The Lover*, 58-65; in *No Man's Land*, 89, 91, 93, 95-98, 100; in *One for the Road*, 125-26; in *Party Time*, 130-32
self-determination, 113

self-development, 45
Sereny, Gitta, 95, 97, 98
Servant, The, 81
Slight Ache, A, 6, 69
Shakespeare, William, 3, 5, 6, 52, 58, 76, 85, 126
Silverstein, Marc, 9, 16, 20, 23, 26, 83, 86, 118, 125, 130, 138
Skelton, John: *Magnifycence*, 13, 30
Space-mind, 2
"Speech of Thanks, A", 7
Speer, Albert, 95, 106, 108
Suter, Anthony, 90, 101
[T]
Taming of the Shrew, The, 15, 29, 83, 86
Taylor, Charles, 3, 51, 63, 65, 92
Taylor, John Russell, 1, 2, 64
Tempest, The, 48, 117, 127, 142
Thatcher, Margaret, 128
Thompson, David T., 29, 86
three a's (the Absurd, alienation, anxiety), 3, 27, 28, 89, 90, 99, 100, 112, 138, 139
Time-mind, 3, 79, 81, 88, 90, 92
1 Timothy, 16
[U]
Udal: *Respublica*, 13, 30
ultimate One, 6, 42
[V]
Van Gogh, Vincent: *A Pair of Boots*, 39, 40
Vice, the, 13
[W]
Wellwarth, George E., 65
Wilde, Oscar, 44, 45, 48
Wind, Edgar, 6, 75, 78, 84
Winter's Tale, The, 43, 48
Wixton, Christopher, 105
Wolfit, Donald, 78, 86, 118
"Writing for Myself", 1, 107

"Writing for the Theatre", 1, 35, 48, 53, 92
"Writing, Politics and *Ashes to Ashes*", 103, 117, 118, 141, 142
Wycherley, William, 44

【X】
X ray, 2, 51, 55, 57, 59, 64, 67, 68, 74, 75, 81, 85

【Z】
Zola, Émile, 4